P9-AFB-110

I DO! I DO!

PAMELA TOTH

H HARLEQUIN® MONTANA MAVERICKS

Special thanks and acknowledgment are given to Pamela Toth for her contribution to the MONTANA MAVERICKS: STRIKING IT RICH miniseries.

Recycling programs for this product may not exist in your area.

ISBN-13: 978-0-373-41804-6

I Do! I Do!

Copyright © 2007 by Harlequin Books S.A.

This edition published by arrangement with Harlequin Books S.A.

For questions and comments about the quality of this book, please contact us at CustomerService@Harlequin.com.

HARLEQUIN®
www.Harlequin.com

Printed in U.S.A.

When she was growing up in Seattle, *USA TODAY* bestselling author **Pamela Toth** planned to be an artist, not a writer. It was only after her mother, a librarian, gave her a stack of Harlequin romances that Pam began to dream about a writing career. However, her plans were postponed while she raised two daughters and worked full-time. Then fate stepped in. Through a close friend, Pam found a fledgling local chapter of Romance Writers of America, and for the next twenty years she belonged to a close-knit group of published writers while penning romances for several lines at Harlequin. When Pam isn't traveling with her husband, she loves spending time with her two grown daughters, antiquing, gardening, cross-stitching and reading.

To all the friends and fans who have offered me
encouragement over the years.

To my daughters, Erika and Melody,
for their unwavering support.

To my husband, Frank,
for his unconditional love. And for all those dinners
out when a deadline approached.

Prologue

Lizbeth Stanton adjusted the neckline of her low-cut pink top and straightened the waistband of her black leather miniskirt. Sucking in a deep breath, she pushed open the door to the card room at the upscale Thunder Canyon Resort where her fiancé, Dax Traub, was playing poker with his buddies and his brother, DJ.

"Well, hello, boys," she drawled, posing dramatically with one hand on her hip as all six men seated around the table stared up at her.

For a moment, the room was silent except for the scrape of chairs as the Cates brothers rose to their feet.

"Evening, Lizbeth," said Marshall Cates. The doctor's cocky grin, handsome as that of a soap opera star's, sent a shiver of feminine appreciation through Liz. She had dated him a few times, but they'd never been serious. His younger brother Mitchell stood silently beside him. If he smiled more often, Mitch might be even better looking than Marshall. Liz had a weakness for black hair and dark eyes.

"Oh, don't get up on my account," she exclaimed with a trace of sarcasm as her gaze swept past them to the others, her fiancé included, who were still seated as though their butts were glued to their chairs.

Reluctantly they, too, stood up. Russ Chilton and Liz's boss, Grant Clifton, wore faintly disapproving expressions. Everyone knew that Russ's attitude toward women was a century behind the times, but Grant was usually happier to see her.

Perhaps she shouldn't have come, but she had wanted to remind Dax of just what he was missing by insisting on spending his evening with the guys instead of with her. Especially when she had the night off from her job tending bar here at the resort.

"I had to check my schedule, so I thought

I'd just say hi," she explained, giving each man her most flirtatious smile. If Grant doubted her excuse, he didn't comment, but both of them knew that she worked a set shift, alternating weekly between days and evenings.

"Well, if it isn't the second most beautiful woman in Montana," exclaimed DJ with a pointed glance at his brother. Their sibling rivalry had resulted in a fist fight at the grand opening of DJ's restaurant a few weeks before. According to Dax, they'd buried the hatchet after that—and not in each other's skulls. Tonight he ignored DJ's dig.

"Could you be just a little biased since you finally talked the beautiful Allaire into marrying you?" Marshall asked, peering at DJ.

It was one of those weird coincidences, probably the result of living in a small town, that Dax had proposed to Liz right after DJ and Allaire, Dax's ex-wife, had announced their engagement. Obviously people who said that Dax was still carrying a torch were wrong.

Liz waited for him to insist that *she* was prettier, but he remained stubbornly silent, arms folded across his chest and a frown on his handsome face. It was Mitch Cates who finally came to her defense.

"Of course Allaire's very pretty," he said with his attention fixed on his pile of chips, "but comparing a blonde to a redhead is like choosing between a delicate flower and a fireworks display. They're both beautiful, but each in its own way."

"What a sweet thing to say," she replied with a reproving glance at Dax. "Thank you, Mitchell."

His dark eyes flicked up to meet hers for an instant as red color stained his cheeks. How could such a brilliant and successful businessman still be so shy, especially around his former high school buddies? He was one male she found impossible to read.

"Dax, I think someone just compared your lady to a firecracker," drawled Russ. "Should we congratulate you or send our condolences?"

Just because Liz had dated a few other men in town before accepting Dax's proposal, Russ had a low opinion of her that he didn't bother to hide. As far as she was concerned, he needed to loosen up.

"What he's saying is that I'm hot and Dax is a lucky man," she replied even though Russ hadn't been speaking to her. She tossed her head so that her earrings would sparkle and spikes of hair sticking up from her ponytail would dance. "Dax knows that, don't you, honey?" If he wasn't going to defend her voluntarily, she'd put him on the spot so he had no choice.

For a moment, he leaned back in his chair and stared steadily back at her, his mouth set in a grim line. Then he shocked her by tossing his cards into the middle of the table.

"I fold," he growled, scooping up his paltry little pile of chips and shoving back his chair. "I came to play poker, not to sit around jawing about flowers and fireworks."

Oh, so men didn't talk while they played? Liz thought. Everyone knew they were worse than women when it came to gossip.

No one breathed a word as Dax grabbed his jacket and stalked out of the room. She would sooner streak naked down Main Street than go running after him, even though her cheeks burned when she caught a couple of sympathetic glances.

"Don't mind him," DJ said after Dax had slammed the door behind him. "He's probably just nervous about getting married again."

Or Dax was upset that his brother was going to marry Allaire, the woman *he* was still in love with, after all, Liz thought miserably. She made sure her smile didn't waver.

Either way, it had obviously been a huge mistake to come here tonight. Now all she had to do was to make a graceful exit without bursting into tears.

"He'll be fine once he stops pouting." She made a dismissive gesture that showed off her new manicure. "After all, we firecrackers like a man who can make a few sparks of his own." She paired a little hip shimmy with a suggestive wink.

A couple of the remaining men chuckled appreciatively at her quip and Marshall gave her two big thumbs up.

"He's got his hands full with you, that's for sure," he said with another charming grin of his own. No wonder every woman in town was crazy about him, even though he was head over heels in love with Mia Smith.

"You'd know about that, old boy," Russ muttered just loud enough for Liz to hear.

Grant whacked Russ on the arm. "You look great tonight, Liz," he said firmly.

"Thanks, boss." She needed to get out of here. "I'm going to let you boys go back to your game. See y'all later."

Amid a chorus of hearty goodbyes, she left

the room. "May the best man win," she called over her shoulder. As she walked down the hallway, she pulled her cell phone from her bag and called Dax, intent on demanding an explanation for his outrageous behavior.

no room. "May he be happy," she murmured
over her shoulder. As she looked down the
hallway, she pulled her cell phone from her
bag and called Dave, intent on berating an
explanation for his escapade in Las Vegas [?]

Chapter One

"You're better off without him, Sis," Emily said in a firm voice. "Dax Traub is an idiot if he doesn't know what he's losing. He's not worth another minute of your time."

Even though Liz was still reeling from the shock of her broken engagement, her sister's words made her feel slightly better.

"I think you're biased," Liz protested in a shaky voice.

She'd called Emily as soon as she'd gotten home from meeting Dax at The Rib Shack, DJ's latest addition to his successful restaurant chain. Apparently Dax had figured she wouldn't make a scene if he gave her the bad news in a public place.

At first Liz had been too stunned to speak, too busy trying to absorb words that seemed to have no meaning. Holding back the threat of tears as he'd sat across from her looking uncomfortable. He'd looked anywhere but at her as he'd squirmed in his chair.

When she'd asked him why in a ragged whisper, he had merely shrugged. "It's not you." His face showed more discomfort than regret or sympathy. "I'm sorry."

Still speechless, Liz had gotten to her feet, legs wobbly, and left the restaurant with as much dignity as she could manage. All the way home from town, tears running down her face, she had asked herself why. *Why?* Dax was handsome and sexy, his bad-boy image not hurt in the least by the motorcycle shop he owned. Apparently Liz just wasn't pretty enough or hot enough to hang on to some-one like him.

"He wasn't right for you, honey," Emily continued. "Why on earth did you get en-gaged to him in the first place? You hadn't dated long, had you? Did you even really know him?"

Liz leaned against the kitchen counter of the tiny cabin where she lived, a cabin owned by Emily and her husband. "No, obviously not," she moaned, "but he was so insistent. When he proposed, he wouldn't take no for an answer and I hated to hurt his feelings."

"Oh, honey," Emily said, "now he's hurt yours, the bum. Maybe it's time to start putting yourself first. Getting married isn't your only option, you know."

Good point, Liz thought as she straightened and walked over to the window above the sink. The view of the trees never failed to calm her.

"I guess it's mainly my pride that's hurt," she admitted, realizing that what she said was true. How many men had she dated because it was hard to turn them down, even when she had no real romantic interest in them?

"Did you love him?" Emily asked. "Could you really picture yourself spending the rest of your life with him?"

Liz tried to picture herself with gray hair and bifocals, seated on a Harley with a shawl draped around her shoulders. "Maybe I was more in love with the idea of getting married than I ever was with Dax." After all, hadn't she been planning her wedding since she was a little girl?

At least she hadn't slept with him. She had

wanted to wait and he'd been okay with that. Perhaps *too* okay.

"Truth be told, I don't think he's over his first wife, Allaire," Liz admitted aloud the niggling suspicion she'd refused to acknowledge before, even in her thoughts. As her fingers tightened on her phone, she watched a woodpecker drilling a nearby tree trunk in a quest for insects. "It probably wasn't a coincidence that we got engaged at about the same time she and DJ made their announcement," she admitted.

Emily groaned again. "You poor thing. If he was on the rebound—"

"You know what," Liz interrupted on a fresh burst of determination, "I'm going to get through this and I'll be okay. You'll see."

"I know you will." Emily's tone was instantly hearty—and as phony as the counterfeit twenty Liz had gotten stuck with at the bar last week.

Still, Liz appreciated her sister's support. Even if Emily did sometimes think Liz was a flake just because she had changed jobs a few times—well, maybe more than just a few— as she tried to figure out what she wanted to do until she met the perfect mate and married him.

Didn't most women like her—single, early twenties—want it all, a great career, a wonderful husband and a perfect family? Wasn't that still the American dream?

She rubbed her temple with her free hand. Was she being realistic in thinking it was possible? Perhaps she needed to rethink things.

Even though having a man in her life would be nice, like having a sports car, she didn't *need* one. She straightened. Emily was right; she had other options. This could be the first day of a new plan, a new direction.

A brand-new Lizbeth Stanton!

The notion was too fresh to share with her sister. She might remind Liz of all the other times she'd made fresh starts, make her doubt herself.

"Em, I've got to go," Liz said, glancing up at the clock. She had a couple of errands to run before her shift at the bar started. "Thanks, though. You know, for listening and all."

"You sure you're going to be okay?" Emily asked, sounding worried. "I wish I could come and see you, but—"

"No, really," Liz replied. "It's sweet of you to offer, but I'll be fine. I *am* fine," she said with renewed enthusiasm. Let Dax moon over his ex-wife, if that was what he wanted to do. She had better things to occupy her!

"All right, but call anytime, okay? I mean it." Emily didn't sound convinced, but Liz knew she was too busy with her own life and her husband to drop everything and hold Liz's hand.

"I know. I will. Take care." After a few more platitudes and promises to stay in touch, Liz finally ended the call. Part of her wished she'd refrained from confiding her bad news to Emily until she'd thought things through, but she wouldn't have been able to keep it secret forever. In a small town like Thunder Canyon, word had probably already spread like an oil slick.

She tossed her head, red-streaked ponytail bobbing. It had been good to be told that Dax was a rat who didn't deserve her. Perhaps she should have seen it coming—especially the way he'd stalked out of his little poker party after she crashed it. She'd been prepared to forgive his tantrum over a nice lunch. Instead he'd dumped her as coolly as canceling an appointment.

Before she got involved again just because she didn't want to say no and dent some man's fragile ego, maybe she needed to spend a little time figuring out what *she* needed. With a huff of self-righteousness, she grabbed a bottled water from the ancient refrigerator and went into the bedroom to change her clothes for work.

Just because she intended to turn over a new leaf didn't mean she wouldn't care about looking especially hot at the bar tonight. So that everyone who came in to find out if she was devastated could see exactly what Dax Traub had foolishly tossed aside.

Mitchell Cates sat in a corner booth at the Lounge, nursing a beer from some local microbrewery he'd never heard of. It was early yet, too early for the dark-paneled lounge to have more than a couple of other customers.

Broodingly he watched a pair of tourists seated at the bar flirt with the bartender on duty. When she threw back her head and laughed at something one of the men said, Mitch found himself wishing he could make Lizbeth laugh like that. He could almost feel the melting warmth of her smile, see the sparkle of interest in her big dark eyes.

Tonight Lizbeth looked especially gorgeous with her dark red-brown hair piled on top of her head, curls and glittering ribbons bouncing in all directions. She was like a brightly colored bird, full of life and energy. What might be messy or overdone on most women looked just right on her. As did her clingy strapless silver top and short black skirt. How could such a petite body come equipped with legs that went on for miles?

He enjoyed watching them every time she came out from behind the bar. Just thinking about her made his mind shut down and his tongue flop around in his mouth like a trout on a hook. He felt like a kid with his first crush.

Scowling, he watched the two men at the bar get to their feet.

"Aw, come on, baby, loosen up," coaxed the one in the baseball cap, leaning toward Lizbeth as the other tossed some bills onto the bar. "It'll be fun. Trust us."

Shaking her head, she pointed to the older bald man polishing glasses at the far end of the bar. "It wouldn't be fair to Moses if I left."

The man who'd spoken to her glanced around the dim room, gaze sliding past Mitch as though he were invisible.

"It's dead here," he argued with a sweep of his hand. "Old Mose can handle it."

The three of them continued to banter until a gray-haired couple walked in and sat in an empty booth. The man looked over at Lizbeth expectantly.

Bidding goodbye to her rowdy admirers, she went over to take the couple's order. While she was distracted, Mitch took a determined breath and carried his glass to the bar. Ever since he'd heard earlier that she and Dax had broken up, he'd been thinking about approaching her. Rehearsing in his head what he would say when he did. Trying not to think about the fact that she'd dated, albeit briefly, his own charming, witty, successful brother before getting mixed up with Traub.

Mitch had never felt less charming or more nervous than he did now as Lizbeth finally came back after serving the older couple their drinks.

"Mitchell Cates," she said gaily, her dark eyes sparkling just for him. "Can I get you another beer?"

Gut clenching, he barely glanced at his half-full bottle. "I'm good, thanks." His mind went blank. "Slow night," he blurted, forgetting all the clever comments he'd thought out earlier.

If she thought him a dull clod, she didn't

let it show. "It's early yet," she replied agreeably. "Business picks up later."

"When do you get through work?" he asked, scorching heat searing his face. "I, uh, didn't mean that the way it sounded," he added, fumbling. He managed to bump his beer bottle, then caught it before it could spill.

She shook her head. The subdued lighting made the red streaks in her hair shimmer. "Don't worry, Mitchell." Reaching across the bar, she patted his hand. "I didn't take it wrong."

He felt that brief touch all the way up his arm and down to his toes. It probably kicked up his blood pressure as it loosened his tongue. Now or never.

Lizbeth glanced past him as another customer walked by. "Good night, Mr. Sinclair," she called before shifting her attention back to Mitch. "I'll be right back."

He turned to admire the sassy twitch of her hips as she collected the check, wiped the table and picked up the dirty glass. Dumping it behind the bar, she came back to where he sat.

He wiped his damp hands on his thighs. "Do you like working here?" he asked. She certainly got on well with the customers, sometimes too well.

She shrugged, making her gold hoop earrings dance. "It's better than my last job at the accounting office." She rolled her eyes expressively. "Bor-ing."

Mitch joined in her laughter. As long as they talked about jobs and careers, he was on solid ground. His was the world of a businessman who'd built his company from one idea, one clever invention, into a brand that was well-known in ranching and farming circles throughout the country and beyond.

When he attempted to cross over to the other side—the social arena of small talk and flirting—he stepped into quicksand. And never more so than when he talked to Lizbeth.

"Have you ever thought about changing jobs?" he asked, hoping desperately for a few more moments alone with her before more thirsty customers showed up.

There was more than one way to get to know someone. Especially someone as appealing as Lizbeth, idly tracing figure-eights on the surface of the bar carved from walnut burl.

Since her world unnerved him so badly, he hoped to bring her into his.

From her surprised expression when she looked up, he realized he'd managed to throw her a curve. "I think about working somewhere else all the time," she admitted with a wary glance at Moses. "I've already changed jobs so many times that I just didn't know if it would be a good idea again unless something really perfect came along."

He ignored the sudden feeling of hesitancy. "So you might be open to suggestions?"

She batted her long lashes, clearly not thinking he was serious. "Just what did you have in mind?"

He resisted the temptation to let his attention wander from her smoky brown eyes to her sweet, full lips. "A legitimate job offer," he replied. "I promise."

Liz studied Mitchell Cates, trying to figure out his game. She got hit on all the time in this job, but he didn't seem the type. He came across as clever, driven, reserved—and every bit as handsome as his brother Marshall. Especially when Mitch smiled as he was doing right now.

Maybe he was more of a player than she'd first thought. She doubted he did his employment recruiting in bars.

Curious, she rested her elbows on the polished wood slab. "I guess it wouldn't hurt to listen," she replied, ignoring the inexplicable feeling of disappointment that he was probably just like other guys.

At least he was someone to talk to. Once the room started jumping, she and the staff coming on in an hour would be lucky for a moment to breathe between drink orders.

"Are you familiar with my company, Cates International?"

"Sure. You make tractors, don't you?" She'd driven past the large complex at the edge of town without paying much attention. With her new plan to put herself first, she needed to make a habit of recognizing opportunities, no matter how unlikely.

Especially one involving a dark-haired man with a killer—if fleeting—smile. Damn, but her old habits were hard to break!

"Tractors," Mitchell echoed. "Close enough, I guess. We actually manufacture hydraulic tables to lift and immobilize cattle. We call them cow-tippers." He shook his head with a rueful grin. "This is where your eyes start to glaze over and you stifle a yawn."

Faking interest in some manly subject she found drop-dead boring was a skill Liz had perfected in adolescence. Gaze unflinching, she pretended fascination. "But why would anyone want to tip a cow?"

"Good question," Mitchell said.

The phone behind the bar began to ring. She glanced at Moses, but he was restocking the Kentucky bourbon. "Excuse me for a moment," she said.

Mitchell nodded. "No problem." While he sipped beer that must surely be warm and flat, she took the call and recited their hours by rote.

"Sorry about that," she said after she'd hung up. "You were talking about tipping cows?"

"Actually, lifting and immobilizing them for various reasons, like trimming their hooves," he explained. "I won't bore you with the sales pitch right now." He slid his beer bottle a couple inches to the right, then moved it back to where it had been. "The thing is that I'm looking for an office assistant. Suzy's leaving, so I'll need someone to answer the phone, keep track of my appointments and do some other office chores."

Liz's interest surged, but then doubt intruded. "How do you know that I can even use a computer?" she asked.

"You just said you worked in an accounting office," he reminded her. "I doubt the basics are much different. What you don't know, you can probably learn. People skills can't be taught and from what I've observed, yours are excellent."

The compliment was gratifying, especially since it had nothing to do with her face or her boobs. How long had it been since someone had recognized her worth in some other less-obvious way than her looks?

He'd certainly snagged her attention, but she wasn't about to be swept off her feet.

"The work here is easy and the tips are good," she countered. "Most of the time, it's a lot of fun." Never mind the aching feet, rude drunks, occasional pinches and pats, and weekend shifts. "Still, a change of pace might be nice."

"Why don't you come on in to the office one morning this week and fill out an application?" he suggested. "We can talk some more."

It was time to up the ante and see if he was serious, since in her experience most men seemed only to want what they couldn't have.

"If I were to really consider leaving the re-sort, it would be for more than just another dead-end job," she explained as a party of four wandered in and sat around a nearby table.

"I'll be right with you," Liz called to them. "Speaking of work," she told Mitch, "I'd better get back to it."

"Finish what you were saying first," he urged her with a brief touch on her wrist, "about what you're looking for?"

Ignoring again her flare of awareness of him as a man—an attractive, successful, available man, as the old Liz would have noticed first and foremost—she stuck to her new resolution.

"I'm looking for a career opportunity," she said firmly, "a genuine chance to move up in the world."

She figured he might laugh in her face as he got to his feet. Imagine someone like her telling a successful entrepreneur like him that he'd have to do better with his offer!

His brown eyes—lighter than Marshall's and shaded with gold—narrowed for an instant and then he took out his wallet. After he'd extracted a couple of bills, he slid a business card toward her.

"Come and see me," he urged again. "We'll talk."

Bemused, she watched him walk purpose-
fully from the Lounge without a backward
glance and then she stared down at the card.
Since his gaze hadn't once wandered to her
cleavage, perhaps his offer really was different from most.

Cates International, read the card in green
script on an ivory background. *Mitchell
Cates, President,* followed by his numbers.

The sound of snapping fingers distracted
her.

"Hey, cutie, shake your booty." A trio of
young guys had come in without her notice. Seated at the bar, all three sniggered as
though they had just invented humor.

Liz plastered a smile on her face. "Down,
boys," she teased. "I'll be right with you."
And if you don't think I'll card you, she promised silently, *think again.*

Mitch looked up from a purchase order he'd
been scanning to see Suzy, the office temp,
standing in the doorway.

"Lizbeth Stanton is here. She said you
asked her to come by, so do you have time to
see her now?" she asked.

He had himself convinced that she probably wouldn't come, especially after she'd told

him her accounting job had been boring. How exciting was farm equipment if you weren't a farmer?

"Bring her right in," he said impatiently as he got to his feet. Did he think she would turn around and leave again if he kept her waiting for more than ten seconds?

He barely had time to smooth down his hair before Suzy reappeared with Lizbeth, who hovered in the doorway while Suzy handed him her résumé.

"Have a seat," he urged, hoping his face didn't betray the extent of his pleasure. Inside he was beaming like a kid with a treat.

"I'm glad you could make it," he said as Lizbeth perched on the edge of a chair facing him, her dark skirt almost reaching her knees. With it she wore a tailored blouse and toned-down makeup. Even the tiny hoops in her ears, a far cry from the glittering bangles, seemed to whisper *serious applicant*.

"Anything else?" Suzy asked from the doorway.

"Coffee?" he suggested as he sat back down behind his desk.

"I'm good, thanks," Lizbeth replied, crossing one slim leg over the other.

"Hold my calls," he told Suzy. "Thanks."

After she had shut the door behind her, he set aside Lizbeth's paperwork without a glance.

"Did you have any trouble finding us?" he asked.

The sun that streamed through the window turned her hair a hundred shades of fiery copper. Whether or not the visual feast was her natural color, it emphasized the chocolate brown of her eyes.

"Marshall pointed it out to me once," she replied. As soon as the words were out, she shifted uncomfortably. "I mean…no, I didn't have any trouble."

It was no secret that she had dated his brother before Marshall hooked up with Mia Smith. Hell, Mitch doubted there was any woman in town who hadn't dated Doctor Dazzle, as he sometimes thought of his outgoing sibling.

"Please don't feel uncomfortable, Lizbeth," Mitch reassured her. "I'm aware of what it's like to live in a small town where everybody knows everyone else's business. It's no big deal."

She appeared to relax. "Please call me Liz."

"So how have you been?"

"You've probably heard that I'm no longer

engaged." She stuck out her bare left hand as proof. "Maybe you noticed when you were in the Lounge the other evening."

He hadn't, but he didn't figure that kissing her hand now would be a good idea, so instead he tried to appear sad for her. "I'm sorry it didn't work out." If this had been a fairy tale, his nose would have grown like Pinocchio's for telling such a whopper.

She tossed her head, making her small gold earrings sparkle. "Like you said, it's not a big deal."

He wondered how Dax could bear to lose her, but for once his buddy hadn't said a word.

"Does that have anything to do with your interest in changing jobs?" he asked curiously.

His question seemed to catch her by surprise. Her gaze darted around his office.

"It made me realize that I can't depend on anyone but myself, so it's time to get serious and start working on a career plan like I mentioned the last time we talked. I just wasn't ready to go public with being dumped then."

"Sounds like you've sworn off men," he replied regretfully. Maybe trying to hire her wasn't a good idea after all.

She started to smile flirtatiously, but then her expression sobered. "I'm putting myself first," she said firmly. "I want to be independent, to take care of myself instead of relying on some man." She leaned forward with a touch of earnestness. "I'm willing to work hard and learn all I can. What I'm asking in return is that you give me a genuine opportunity. I'm done being window dressing."

Mitch had been picturing himself leaning over her shoulder, basking in the scent of her perfume while she gave him a list of his phone calls. Admiring her legs as she perched on the corner of his desk or soaking up the admiration in her big brown eyes when he outlined some new product idea.

Reluctantly, he realized he'd been guilty of the worst kind of chauvinistic fantasies between a boss and his secretary. That attitude was not only wrong, it was unfair, especially when he considered himself a progressive employer who gave his workers respect and loyalty.

In the lengthening silence, Liz had begun to pick at the hem of her skirt. Her chin went up in a gesture he was beginning to recognize as a defensive reaction.

"Perhaps I've misunderstood your offer."

Her voice had cooled, its former enthusiasm gone as she started to rise.

Mitch gestured for her to stay put. "Believe me, my need for a full-time assistant is legitimate," he said insistently. "I'm looking for someone who wants Cates International to be part of her future." He took a deep breath. "Come on. I'll explain more while I show you around."

"I can't believe you're really doing it," Kay Costner, Liz's closest friend in Thunder Canyon, said from the next chair as Shandie Solomon spun Liz around to face the mirror.

"What do you think?" Shandie asked Liz as the they both studied her reflection. Shandie had recently begun working at the beauty shop and Liz liked her youthful attitude as well as her knowledge of trendy styles.

Liz studied her hair with mixed feelings. "It's funny," she replied as she tipped her head first one way and then another. "Last week I was thinking about adding scarlet or purple streaks and now I look more—"

"Like a secretary?" Kay supplied.

"Like a serious professional person," Liz corrected her. She met Shandie's gaze in the glass. "It's perfect."

A few minutes later, as Liz and Kay walked to their cars, Kay looked her up and down with a considering expression. "I hope this new job will make you happy," she said with a sincere tone. "Dax is a rat, but I'm worried that you're overreacting."

Liz grinned at her friend. "You mean because I've quit my job as a bartender, undergone a complete makeover and maxed out my credit card on a new professional wardrobe?" she asked teasingly.

"That, too, I guess," Kay replied with an airy gesture. "I was actually referring to the neutral polish color on your nails. Not a rhinestone or a butterfly in sight."

As Liz gave her a playful shove, they both laughed. "Fun-ny," Liz replied. "When a girl is starting a new phase of her life, she needs to look the part."

"And, girl," Kay said as they high-fived each other, "you're gonna knock your boss's socks off."

"All I want to do is to show him that I take this opportunity very seriously," Liz reminded her. "And that I'm a complete professional."

She glanced at her reflection in an adjacent storefront window, cropped top under her denim jacket, tight jeans and high-heeled leather boots. "Yes!" she exclaimed, reaching up her arms as she shimmied her hips, tipped back her head and shouted, "I am woman, hear me roar!"

With a last enthusiastic whoop, she spun in a wobbly circle just in time to see her future boss getting into his truck right across the empty street.

If she'd had any doubt that he had missed her little show, the wave of his hand before he shut his door dispelled it.

Chapter Two

Mitch sat in his leather office chair frowning at the invitation to DJ Traub's wedding. It wasn't that Mitch begrudged DJ the happiness of marrying a woman he so obviously loved—it was just that he hated attending social functions by himself.

He slipped the invitation back into its matching envelope and tossed it into the top drawer of his desk. Glancing impatiently at the clock on the opposite wall, which had been made from a thin slice of Montana granite, he slid back his chair and got to his feet.

This was Lizbeth's first day and she would

be here at any moment. Convincing her to come to work for him hadn't been easy, but she'd finally agreed to give her notice at the Lounge.

Mitch hadn't been surprised to get an angry phone call that same day from Grant, accusing him of stealing the best bartender on staff. Lucky for Mitch that his friendship with Clifton went back far enough that the other man had calmed down almost immediately, even though he had acquired the reputation of being a real hard-ass. With a knowing chuckle, Grant even warned him about getting involved with a woman like Liz.

"It's strictly business," Mitch had replied without a twinge of guilt, "but if I do need dating advice, I'll be sure to come to you first."

It was no secret among the guys that Grant himself had at one time pretended a romantic interest in Lizbeth in order to make Stephanie Julen jealous. Perhaps he'd forgotten his little ploy, since he persuaded Steph to marry him, but Mitch hadn't.

Restlessly, he sat back down and picked up a trade magazine. He was flipping through the pages when Suzy's perky voice came over

his intercom. She'd agreed to stay on for a few
more days until Liz was comfortable.

"Boss, you said to let you know when Ms.
Stanton arrived. She's getting out of her Jeep
right now."

"Okay, thanks." As he got to his feet and
circled his desk, he could feel the same adrenaline rush he got whenever he began a new
project. Well, in a crazy way, getting to know
Lizbeth better on his own turf was a project
of sorts, one he hoped would become a rous-
ing success.

By the time he walked down the short
hallway to the reception area adjacent to the
showroom, Lizbeth was coming through the
glass front door. Even though he recognized
her, he nearly did a double-take.

The brightly colored butterfly who had previously captured his attention had evolved
into a dull brown moth.

Lizbeth must have noticed his expression,
because her smile faded. "I was supposed to
start today, wasn't I?" she asked hesitantly.
"I thought you said to come in on Monday."

Mitch gathered his scattered wits and hurried forward, hand extended. "Of course,"
he exclaimed with a heartiness that sounded

false to his own ears. "You're right on time, isn't she, Suzy?"

The younger girl bobbed her head. "Absolutely," she agreed with an uncomplicated grin. "We start work at eight sharp."

Lizbeth appeared relieved as she slipped off her tan coat. "Is there somewhere I can put this?"

"Shall I show her?" Suzy asked Mitch while he wondered what had happened to the brightly streaked auburn hair that was currently fastened into a tidy knot on top of Lizbeth's head. Its severity went all too well with her dark brown jacket, matching slacks and low-heeled shoes, all proof of just how seriously she took her new job.

She was still beautiful, especially when she smiled, but he'd grown fond of her more eccentric appearance. It seemed like part of her personality, so perhaps that would be more subdued as well. He was curious to find out.

"No, that's okay," he told Suzy, who waited expectantly. "I'll show her." He indicated that his new assistant proceed him down the hall. "This way."

After Lizbeth had hung up her coat, he introduced her to the bookkeeper, who handed her some payroll forms to fill out.

"When she's done, bring her to my office," he told Nita. If the older woman thought it was odd that Mitch was showing Lizbeth around personally, she didn't let on. After all, it was a small office and Liz was going to report directly to him.

"Sure thing," she said instead, handing Lizbeth a pen.

Once he was back behind his desk, Mitch swiveled his chair around so he could stare out the window at the view of jagged mountains. The sight never failed to remind him of his relative insignificance compared to such timeless grandeur. In the face of it, whatever he was wrestling with usually shrunk to manageable proportions.

Today the view barely registered as he stared blindly. Had he forgotten that this butterfly he'd hoped to impress with his success was a real person, with desires and ambitions of her own? Had he given a thought to what she might want when he had concocted this harebrained scheme?

A knock on his open door interrupted his silent self-condemnation. Swapping out his frown for a more welcoming expression, he got to his feet.

"Lizbeth, come on in," he invited.

"Remember, I prefer Liz if you don't mind," she said softly. "And what should I call you now that you're my boss?"

"I'm still just Mitch," he replied. "We're a pretty informal bunch here and a few of my people have been with me since the beginning."

"I hope you'll have the time to tell me about it." She hovered just inside the door, hands clasped loosely in front of her.

Silently he reminded himself that she was probably trying to make a few points, but that she wouldn't really be interested in the details of how he'd built Cates International from the ground up.

"For now let's take a quick look at the shop," he suggested. "I'll introduce you to the foreman and the warehouse manager."

By the time Liz got home to her sister's cabin that evening, she was tired but elated. Everyone she'd met today seemed so nice. Especially Mitch.

As far as she knew, he was still single. The old Liz would have been focused on getting him to ask her out. Resisting his tall, dark and possibly dangerous appeal wasn't going to be easy, but she was determined to keep this relationship professional.

After she had set down her purse and the bag from the local teriyaki takeout, she hung her new coat on a hook next to the door. The cabin didn't provide any closets, just a tiny wardrobe in the single bedroom. Maybe someday she would move into town, but giving up the quiet setting and spectacular scenery wouldn't be easy unless her sister and brother-in-law decided that they wanted the cabin for themselves. Meanwhile, Liz intended to focus all of her energy on learning everything she could about Cates International.

Liz's third day on the job was her first without Suzy running interference. So far her duties had been light. Despite what Mitch had told her previously, if he was around he usually answered his own phone and took care of his own e-mails. She was beginning to wonder if there would be enough work to keep her busy.

When he came down the hall from his office, she was studying their catalog. Unlike yesterday when he'd been dressed in a dark gray suit for his meeting with the manager of the local bank, today he wore snug jeans and a green knit shirt. On the chest pocket, the company name was stitched in gold. The shirt was just like the one she had seen Nita wearing on Monday, except that on Mitch it looked a hundred times better.

She tried to ignore the sizzle of awareness. For a businessman, he was in great shape. Before she had thought of him as a somber, rather shy individual who came into the lounge for an occasional beer. Now she realized that while he lacked Marshall's outgoing, sometimes overwhelming charisma, Mitch's quiet confidence was in its own way even more appealing.

"How's it been going?" he asked when he saw her. "Are you doing okay?"

"I feel guilty for not working harder," she admitted.

A couple of times in the last two days she had caught him studying her with a speculative expression. She was used to having men watch her, but not the way Mitch did, as though he was trying to figure out what made her tick. She had yet to decide if it made her uncomfortable.

"Don't worry about not having enough to do," he said. "You'll more than make up for it before the trade shows." One of the things he'd asked was whether she minded working overtime or traveling on business. For some reason, it hadn't occurred to her that she might be accompanying him on those trips.

"Is it okay if I help Nita?" she asked. "I saw a stack of filing in her office."

He shrugged, thumbs hooked into his wide leather belt. "Sure, that would be fine. Before you do, though, I was going to show you my shop."

Liz grinned up at him, nearly batting her eyes from sheer habit. "Have you forgotten that you showed me the shop on my first day?"

The term didn't begin to describe the large manufacturing floor where several workers had been busy assembling one of the various models of the Cates "cow-tipper."

Mitch cocked his head as an answering smile spread to his eyes, making them glow from within. "Ah, that's true, but you haven't seen my personal shop, though."

"That's where the miracles happen," Nita exclaimed in a dry voice that startled Liz. Mitch must not have heard her approach either, because he seemed to jerk away from Liz's desk and color stained his cheeks.

"Miracles?" Liz echoed, looking from one to the other with a questioning expression.

If Nita had been closer to Mitch's age, Liz might have wondered if the two shared a history that included more than merely business. She must be imagining things.

"My shop is where I tinker," he explained. "Where I work on new ideas."

Liz had known from reading the company history on their Web site that Mitch had an engineering background, but she hadn't really pictured him doing any of the actual creating.

"I'd like to see it," she replied.

"Nita, did you need something?" Mitch asked as Liz pushed back her chair and got to her feet.

"I was going to ask Liz for her size so we can order her some company shirts. They take a couple of weeks to get here."

His gaze flickered over her body, then at his own feet. "Not my area of expertise," he muttered, his sudden discomfiture reminding her of the way he'd usually acted when she waited on him at the resort. "Uh, I forgot something in my office," he continued. "Be right back."

As he hurried away, Liz and Nita exchanged amused glances. "I love it when he gets rattled," Nita said in a low voice, looking extremely pleased. "He's a great guy and it doesn't happen often, but sometimes he needs to have his control tweaked."

"Most of the guys I've known would offer to do the measuring personally," Liz replied dryly. "And I wear a medium."

"Okay." Nita shook her head. "Mitch isn't that way. I've been here since the beginning and I've never seen him cross that line. Everyone who works here knows that kind of thing isn't tolerated." She glanced over her shoulder, lowering her voice even more. "Trust me, his first love is the business. You don't have a thing to worry about in that department."

Nita's words should have reassured the new and improved Liz, but what she felt was disappointment. Was she attracted to him despite her best efforts?

"Good to know," she replied calmly just as he reappeared.

"To know what?" he asked.

"I was just telling her that the medical insurance takes effect in thirty days," Nita replied innocently. "Well, I've got to get back to work or the boss will be after me." She winked at Liz. "I'll order your shirts. Let me know if you have any more questions about the benefits package."

"Sure thing," Liz replied. "Thanks."

"Okay, shall we go?" Mitch held open the heavy door to the manufacturing area with its noisy machines, loud music and raised voices. Just inside the door was a rack holding hard hats. When she reached for a bright yellow one as she had on her first day, he stretched his hand above her head and took down a green one.

"This is what a Cates employee wears," he said, handing it to her.

Her name was printed in gold above the molded brim.

"Thank you." Cautiously she set it on her upswept hair. Funny how having a hat with her name on it made her feel like one of the team.

As a time clock mounted on the wall next to a rack of cards clicked over, he donned a matching hat that looked slightly beat up. "This way."

Mitch had to bite his tongue to keep himself from telling Lizbeth how cute she looked in her new headgear. He'd thought getting to know her would be easier on his home turf, but she still intimidated him.

Like a little boy showing off a birdhouse he'd constructed from popsicle sticks, he took out a key ring. Unlocking a door in the wall, he led her to the place where his ideas took shape. If she was bored silly, it would probably serve him right for thinking a woman like her would find it—or him—interesting.

Their gazes met as he opened the door and let her go ahead of him. What choice did he have but to try?

"Wow." Slowly she turned in a circle as she looked around the clean, well-lit room. "I expected someplace dark and cluttered, but this looks more like a lab than an inventor's workshop."

His gaze followed hers. On the wall above the spacious counter were assorted hand tools. A rack held blueprints and specs. File cabinets lined the short wall next to a small beat-up desk, bare except for a computer. Across from it was a drafting table. Nothing was out of place.

"I guess I'm a little obsessive when it comes to where I work," he said apologetically.

Great, now she thought he was some kind

of oddball neat freak. He'd hoped she might view him as fascinating and clever, not as the nutty professor.

"I confess, I'm with you," she said, surprising him. "I just can't stand having a lot of *stuff* everywhere. It just makes me crazy." When she leaned closer, the scent he'd learned to associate with her teased his nostrils. "Want to know something?"

"Uh-huh." He bobbed his head.

"I'm a secret organizer," she whispered conspiratorially. "I go crazy in those container stores."

"I…I'll have to check one out," he said.

The door was shut to keep out the noise and dust from the main area. Maybe being alone with her in here wasn't such a good idea.

She looked around curiously, her slim hands resting on her hips. Today she wore navy blue slacks and a man-tailored light blue shirt that failed to disguise her curves. Even now, more simply dressed and wearing little if any cosmetics, she made his breath catch.

He'd be in serious trouble if he had to spend forty plus hours a week in a constant state of awareness, with the blood flow to his brain seriously diminished.

"What does this do?" she asked, indicating a small drill press.

Briefly he explained. "Most of the actual machining is done out there. No point in duplicating equipment."

"You love it, don't you?" she guessed. "All this, it's not just a job, a business. It's a passion with you."

"Everyone should work at what they love," he replied. "What good is success if you aren't happy?"

"Exactly!" She looked pleased. "That's what I want, to feel that way about what I do and to work at a job I believe in."

He studied her, reminded that there was more to her than dark flashing eyes and a shape to make a man weep. "Do you think you can find that here, or is it too soon to tell?"

When she grinned, he pretended it was for the man and not the boss.

"I'm hoping," she replied. "I guess we'll find out."

He thought about tossing caution aside and kissing her, but he'd never gained anything worthwhile by plunging ahead without a plan. Glad she couldn't read his mind, he took her back to the office, breathing a sigh of relief when the reception desk was safely between them.

"I suppose you know that DJ and Allaire are getting married on Friday," he began cautiously.

She took her seat, looking up at him warily. "Yes, I'd heard." Something flickered in her eyes, making him wonder if she was over her broken engagement to Dax.

"He's been my friend for a long time," Mitch continued, "so I can't miss it."

Liz's expression lost some of its wariness. "Of course not," she echoed. "It should be a nice ceremony. I overheard at the beauty shop that Allaire's going with a Parisian theme."

"What the heck does that mean?" he blurted, genuinely puzzled. How did women come up with stuff like that? "A cake shaped like the Eiffel Tower?"

Liz burst into laughter. "I truly haven't a clue. You'll have to let me know."

Under the circumstances, he wasn't surprised that she hadn't been invited. "They're keeping it kind of small," he explained hastily as a car door slammed out front.

He looked out the window. Damn, he'd forgotten all about his appointment with the rep from the new graphics company. It was local, which he preferred.

"That must be Jim Parks from Mountain Art," Liz said after she'd glanced at her notepad. "Do you want to duck into your office real quick so I can show him back?"

What rotten timing.

"No, not necessary," Mitch replied as the salesman, gray-haired with glasses, entered the building. "Jim," he exclaimed, extending his hand. "I'm Mitchell Cates. Come on in."

Liz didn't talk to Mitch again all afternoon. Since she had nothing else to do, she did some research about the business on the Web. At least she might be able to ask Mitch some intelligent questions.

She saw the rep walk around from the main shop and get into his car, but her boss wasn't with him. There was only so much a person could retain about farm equipment at one sitting and Nita was busy compiling a report. Time dragged.

Liz finally went to Mitch's office on the pretext of asking if he wanted coffee, but he wasn't in. On a sideboard rested a photo of his poker group seated around a picnic table. It was the same guys who had been at the party she'd crashed; Mitch, Marshall, Russ, Grant, DJ and Dax.

For a moment, she stared down at the picture. Not wanting to get caught prowling Mitch's office, she went back out to her desk, but her mind stayed on Dax, her former fiancé. If he was already seeing someone else, Liz hadn't heard about it yet.

With a sudden burst of insight, she realized that she didn't care. Dax had wounded her pride, but not her heart. She hadn't loved him, not really. Aside from the embarrassment of being rather publicly dumped, Liz owed him a debt of gratitude. If not for their breakup, she might have eventually found herself in a loveless marriage. She wouldn't have realized that she deserved more out of life than Dax could give her. She certainly wouldn't have embarked on a new career path.

Not when her main goal had been a big fancy wedding with the perfect dress, tons of flowers and all the rest of the pomp and circumstance that went with it. For years she had spent untold hours reading bridal magazines and looking at Web sites, studying rings and bridesmaid dresses, bouquets and cakes.

She had pictured the actual event so many

times in her head that it almost seemed real. She could see herself floating up the length of white carpet toward the altar. In the glow of a thousand candles, she struggled to see her groom's face clearly, tall and dark—

"Ah, I'm glad you're still here," Mitch exclaimed, startling her out of her daydream. "I wanted to ask…about DJ's wedding…would you go with me?"

Chapter Three

Liz stared up at Mitch, who had appeared beside her desk while she was daydreaming. "You want me to go with you to DJ and Allaire's wedding?" she echoed.

"I'd like that very much," he replied quietly. "Please say yes."

His steady gaze and half-smile were somehow much more appealing to Liz than his brother Marshall's easy charm had ever been. When she looked at Mitch, it was hard to remember what she'd ever seen in his brother, even though he was a great guy.

For a moment, she was tempted to accept, but then she remembered her resolution. Reluctantly she shook her head.

"I appreciate the offer, but I don't think it's a good idea for us to go out," she said reluctantly. "I hope you understand."

He folded his arms across his chest. "Mind if I ask why?"

Oh, darn. She might have guessed that a man as successful as Mitch wouldn't easily take no for an answer. Part of his formula for success must be persistence.

Liz tended to have a difficult time standing her ground when it came to persistence. She had a tough time—at least to a certain extent—saying no to people. She was always afraid of hurting their feelings, which was why she'd gone out with a number of men she hadn't found at all attractive.

With a burst of insight, she suddenly realized that her difficulty in saying no was exactly why she had ended up engaged to Dax. *Not* because she'd really been in love with him.

Lesson learned.

Despite the injection of fresh determination, she was still hesitant. What if Mitch didn't understand?

"I've decided to focus my energy on doing a good job here," she explained gently, hands clasped tightly on her lap beneath her desk.

She could see that saying no without guilt was going to take some practice. "I just think dating my boss could complicate that, don't you?"

Mitch's golden brown eyes narrowed, giving her a glimpse of the strength behind his success as he studied her as though she were some new kind of mechanical gizmo he'd never seen before. Then his expression cleared.

"Oh, I get it." He chuckled lightly. "You thought I was asking you on a *date*."

Oops. "Weren't you?" she squeaked, sudden embarrassment nearly choking her.

He held out his hands, palms up. "My fault entirely. I know you're probably still getting over what happened with Dax, but I should have explained myself better."

The last thing she wanted was for Mitch or anyone else to think she was carrying a torch for Dax Traub. "It's not that at all," she protested.

"Look, DJ is one of my best friends," he continued earnestly as though she hadn't even spoken. "There's no way I could skip his nuptials, but I hate showing up stag. It's just so awkward, you know? Brides see a single guy at a wedding and right away they start think-

ing about who they could fix him up with."
He shook his head slowly. "I don't get it, but
there it is and I'd really rather avoid the whole
idea." His smile was almost pleading. "We
wouldn't even have to speak to Dax if you
didn't want to, but I'd consider it a huge favor
if you'd go with me."

Liz felt totally, *totally* foolish for jumping
to conclusions. "I understand," she reassured
him, cheeks burning. "Of course I'll go with
you."

"Great." He rubbed his hands together.
"Well, we can work out the details later."

It was only after he'd walked away, whis-
tling tunelessly under his breath, that Liz realized how neatly she'd been boxed in. Not that
he had *meant* to manipulate her, of course. It
was obvious that he had no personal interest
in her. He just wanted someone to hang on
his arm.

The old Liz would have been disappointed,
even wondered what was wrong with her that
he *wasn't* attracted. In some ways being the
new Liz was going to be so much easier!

After glancing at her watch, she cleared
off her desk. Even Career-Woman Barbie, as
she secretly called herself sometimes, would
need to figure out what to wear. On general

principle, it wouldn't hurt to show Dax what he had tossed aside.

With her credit card maxed out from buying a new work wardrobe, she would just have to find something in her closet. Lucky for her that it was well stocked with party clothes.

Through the showroom window, Mitch watched Liz leave for the day. She walked quickly, trim and professional in her charcoal gray slacks and matching jacket. Her hair was gathered into a loose knot.

A small part of him, the randy Neanderthal who responded to hot babes with barely covered curves, missed the sexy bartender. His mature side appreciated her more subdued appearance while he struggled to reject boss-secretary fantasies involving horn-rimmed glasses and spike-heeled shoes.

He'd nearly blown it when he asked her to go to DJ's wedding with him. Good thing he realized his mistake in the nick of time and changed direction. Not that he was a fan of subterfuge or deceit, but neither was he willing to abandon the prize.

Not when the prize was Lizbeth Stanton.

The cell clipped to his belt rang, distracting him. He glanced at the number that was displayed and answered the call.

"Hey, bro," Marshall exclaimed. "We need to nail down the details for DJ's bachelor blowout. Want to grab some dinner at the Hitching Post tonight?"

Mitch hoped his brother's plans didn't run to strippers and X-rated videos. Then again, knowing Marshall, he would have been surprised if they did. Especially now that Marshall had taken the big fall into love, himself.

"Sure thing," Mitch replied, watching Liz's car disappear down the road. "What time did you have in mind?"

To Mitch's way of thinking, DJ's bachelor party was a big success. Under the pretext of hosting a surprise party for another doctor, Marshall had managed to book the latest addition to the groom's own string of restaurants, The Rib Shack, for the evening.

"I never suspected a thing," DJ exclaimed yet again from his place of honor, surrounded by the usual suspects: Mitch, Marshall, Russ and Grant. More of DJ's friends filled the private banquet room, stuffing themselves with barbecue and beer. Only his brother, Dax, was absent.

Marshall, who had given the first toast, turned to high-five DJ. "Don't know what that says about my cleverness or your gullibility, my friend, but I'm glad you're having a good time."

"Enjoy it while you can," drawled Russ, who'd been divorced for years. "Once you take on the ball and chain, you can kiss your freedom goodbye."

Perhaps being estranged from his only child had made Russ bitter. Or maybe it was the changes that had taken place around Thunder Canyon since fresh gold had been found in the old abandoned mine. Russ had made it clear on more than one occasion that he liked the area just fine the way it used to be. Either way, he seemed to have grown even more cynical with time.

"Aw, don't listen to him," Grant told DJ. "Allaire's a sweet lady and she's also *seriously gorgeous*. You're lucky to be with her."

Grant and Russ had been friends for years, but lately they hadn't seemed to get along very well. Tonight, the tension between the two men was almost palpable. Mitch wondered if he was the only one who noticed it.

"Grant's right," he felt compelled to add. "Besides, a lot of marriages turn out just fine."

Marshall dug his elbow into Mitch's arm. "Spoken like a man in love," he taunted. "Who is she, bro? You can tell us."

"You're crazy," Mitch replied. He was relieved when Russ spoke up again, deflecting their friends' attention away from him.

"On the other hand, we all know how clear-headed our boy Grant is," Russ drawled, drawing fresh laughter from the other men seated at the table. "Ever since he hooked up with—"

"Watch it, Chilton," Grant warned, flattening his hands on the table as though he might leap to his feet. "Just because you've sworn off women doesn't make you smarter than the rest of us. Just a hell of a lot more pathetic."

Mitch could tell that he wasn't the only one who suddenly felt uncomfortable. Despite the loud music and raised voices around them, everyone at the table had fallen silent.

Except for Russ. Never one to back down from a perceived challenge, he leaned forward to return Grant's stare.

"I haven't sworn off women, friend." Russ's tone was mocking. "I'm just smart enough to keep from making the same mistake twice."

The tension threatened to explode, but then

it was broken by Grant's chuckle. "I guess time will tell which one of us is the smart one, *friend*."

He got to his feet and looked at the others as though he didn't have a concern in the world. "Who's ready to play pool?"

Liz parked her car in the empty lot in front of Cates International. Mitch had offered to pick her up at the cabin, but she had insisted on meeting him here. Since this wasn't a real date, it seemed to make more sense. Besides, just because he was her boss and she was doing him a favor didn't mean she wasn't attracted to him. Having him drop her off here kept things less personal.

She arrived early, but a sleek silver coupe pulled in moments later. Since Mitch drove a big green pickup to work, she was a little surprised to recognize him behind the wheel of the fancy car.

By the time she had scooped up her purse and opened her door, he was waiting for her.

"You look fantastic," he said, extending his hand. "Elegant and sexy."

She could have echoed his words as she looked up at him. It wasn't the first time she'd seen him in an impeccably tailored dark suit, but tonight the security light was behind him, leaving his face partly in shadow. For an instant, it appeared leaner, more angular, as if his civility had been stripped away.

Jolted, she hesitated, but the warmth of his hand grasping hers reassured her. As she slid from behind the wheel, her leg was bared to midthigh by the short skirt of her party dress under her white wool coat. Tugging at it, she wondered if he noticed.

"Thank you," she murmured.

Wordlessly, he settled her into the leather passenger seat of his Lexus. Before he drove from the lot, he looked at her again. "I'm glad you agreed to come."

She returned his smile without speaking as she smoothed out her skirt. Her nail color was a few shades darker than her red dress, which was one of her favorites. Its flattering style gave her a shot of confidence. A feeling of feminine empowerment.

From Mitch's appreciative expression, she could tell that—like most males—he was influenced by a woman's appearance. Wasn't that what she'd set out to do, to dazzle him and every other man at the wedding?

How could she expect her new boss to focus on her mind and her ability to work hard if she tried to distract him? She couldn't very well have it both ways.

"You're awfully quiet," Mitch said after a few minutes. "Second thoughts?"

"No, of course not," she replied. "Why would you think that?"

He shrugged as he made a left turn. "No one blames you for your broken engagement," he said, surprising her. "Things like that happen."

Dax was sure to be there, despite the fact that his brother was marrying his own ex-wife. What an awkward situation, especially for the bride.

Liz glanced at Mitch, at his strong profile and his hands resting easily on the wheel. Strong, capable hands.

A shiver of awareness went through her. "Dax was a mistake," she blurted. "I'm not carrying a torch, if that's what you think." Did she sound desperate? Defensive?

He grinned without turning his head. "Good to know."

Liz didn't realize they had arrived until he slid the car into a parking spot and came to a stop. All around them, people were headed inside.

"I'll get your door," Mitch said as he got out of the car.

Liz took that to mean he didn't want her to leap out on her own. This wasn't the time to assert her independence, so she curled her fingers around her evening bag and waited.

Mitch hadn't expected to be so moved by a simple wedding ceremony, but the love shining from DJ and Allaire's faces as they exchanged their vows had struck him as something rare and rather precious. Despite all of DJ's grumbling about the plans and choices that went into the event, it served as a reminder of everything two people could find together if they were lucky. What Mitch hoped to find with Liz.

He'd taken her hand during the ceremony and she hadn't objected. As DJ and his bride came up the aisle, Mitch's grip tightened for a moment before he let go. His buddies' lives were changing before his eyes, making him eager to experience the same kind of happiness, himself.

"That was nice," Liz said a few moments later when they walked toward the reception hall. "They looked sweet together."

"I don't know if DJ would appreciate being called sweet," Mitch replied, "but I can't say I've ever seen him this happy before."

Up ahead of them, he saw his brother with Mia Smith. Marshall had confided a while ago that he had fallen for the newcomer to Thunder Canyon. He'd further surprised Mitch by adding that Liz had been partly responsible for getting him to ask Mia out. Since that was when she and Marshall were dating, Mitch assumed there must not have been any sparks between them.

Mitch hadn't done a very good job in hiding his own interest in her from Marshall. Lucky for Mitch, Marshall had been too wrapped up in Mia at the time to notice.

Apparently that was still the case, as Marshall smiled down at Liz without noticing Mitch right behind her. Dark-haired Mia had a self-assured air about her, as though she had grown up surrounded by wealth and privilege, but Mitch knew differently.

With her arm linked through his, Liz hesitated in the doorway. "Oh, how pretty," she exclaimed over the sound of music from within. "I've never been to Paris, but this is just the way I picture it."

Once they were inside, Mitch glanced around the room that had been transformed into a French bistro. Grapevines had been wrapped around the pillars and there were posters of the Eiffel Tower, the Seine River and the Arc de Triomphe on the walls. The wait staff all wore red-striped tops and black pants. At each end of the buffet table were French flags. Even the music had a vaguely French flavor, aided by the squeeze-box being played by one of the band members.

People were lined up at the bar, milling around or standing in small groups as they waited for the bride and groom to reappear. Mitch recognized most of the other guests, but he assumed that Liz might not. Unless she'd served them drinks at the resort, of course. Or dated them, he thought with a frown.

His line of thought was interrupted when she unbuttoned her coat. "I'd like to hang this up," she said as he slid it from her shoulders.

When she turned to face him, her coat almost dropped from his suddenly nerveless fingers. He had always known she was gorgeous, but apparently her sedate appearance at work had lulled him into forgetting that she was downright smokin' hot.

The fire-engine-red dress that bared her shoulders and flared out around her long, long legs was one of hell of a reminder. For a moment, all Mitch could do was stare.

"Holy mother of Mary," whispered a man who was standing nearby. "Is she the entertainment?"

Liz's cheeks turned the same shade as her dress and Mitch glared at the beefy, balding stranger who had made the comment. From the man's dazed expression and his empty glass, it was obvious that he had already visited the bar.

As Mitch tensed, Liz tugged on his arm. "Please," she urged him in a low voice, "don't say anything and make a scene. It happened all the time at the bar, I'm used to it."

Before he could reply, a door at the far end of the room opened and DJ and Allaire appeared, greeted by cheers, applause and whistles. Mitch realized that his reaction to the drunk had been more possessive than he had any right to be. Not yet, anyway.

"I'm sorry," he said softly to Liz. "You look fantastic and you certainly don't deserve to be insulted." Although it went against his nature to stand helplessly aside while she—or any woman—was being mistreated, he realized that taking any action would only serve to embarrass her further.

While DJ made a little speech, thanking everyone for coming, Mitch rested his hands protectively on her bare, silky shoulders. He could feel her tension, so he squeezed gently, tempted to lean closer and inhale her scent. Before he could lose his head and nuzzle her neck, he came to his senses. Luckily, no one seemed to be paying the slightest attention.

"Would you like something to eat or drink?" he suggested as DJ and Allaire were surrounded by well-wishers. "We might as well wait a bit for the crowd to thin before saying hello."

Liz shifted so she could look up at him with her big brown eyes. "I'm starving," she replied with a slight smile. "Let's check out the buffet."

While Liz helped herself to shrimp and pasta salad from the buffet table, she could still feel the warm imprint of Mitch's hands on her shoulders. Even though she knew he hadn't meant for her to read anything into the gesture, it made her feel special.

Waiting for the line to move, she glanced back at him and smiled. All the times he'd come into the bar when she was working, why hadn't she ever paid attention to him? Had she been too addicted to bad boys to notice him?

"Thanks for inviting me," she said when he lifted his brows in silent query.

A warm grin lit up his lean face. "I'm glad you said yes."

When their plates were full, she looked around for somewhere to sit. He probably wanted to join one of the laughing groups of people he knew, but having either dated a few of the men or served them at the Gallatin Room didn't exactly make her feel as though she'd be welcome.

"There's an empty table," Mitch said, pointing. "Let's grab it."

After he had pulled out her chair and asked what she wanted to drink, he went to the bar. While she waited for him, Liz looked around to see what the other women were wearing. Some of the dresses showed a lot more skin than hers, and more than one plunging neckline should have been secured with double-back tape. A couple of the skirts were short enough to double as skating outfits and some of the bling had to be real.

Wait till she described everything to Kay. Her friend hadn't bothered to hide her envy when Liz told her she was coming.

"I want to hear every detail," Kay had insisted. "Dresses, food, the whole works. Don't let your hunky date distract you from the important stuff or I'll be upset!"

Now Liz watched Mitch work his way toward her with a glass in each hand. Several people greeted him, but he didn't stop to talk.

At one point a high-maintenance blonde with a fake tan snagged his arm. Liz recognized her as a frequent customer at the Lounge who liked her booze—and often forgot to leave tips. When he gestured toward the table where Liz waited, the other woman sent her a dismissive glance, but he managed to extricate himself without spilling either drink.

Briefly he spoke to Grant Clifton, whose arm was around a woman Liz knew from the riding stable. Stephanie gave lessons there, but tonight she had shed her casual clothes for a green halter dress that played up the sun streaks in her pretty blond hair. With them was Riley Douglas, Grant's boss at the resort, and his wife, Lisa. The couple owned a local mine called The Queen of Hearts. Everyone had thought it was played out until a new vein of gold had been discovered in a bizarre series of events just a couple of years ago.

Liz wondered what it would be like to have

that much money. "Do you know everyone here?" she asked when Mitch finally sat down beside her.

He shrugged. "I suppose. I probably went to school with most of them. It's funny," he added, "but people get so busy with their lives that you can live in the same town and never see them, except for times like these."

"DJ and Allaire seem so happy," Liz murmured, squirming when she realized how wistful she sounded. If she wasn't careful, Mitch would think her main intention was to snag the boss.

"Took them long enough to sort things out," he replied between bites. "DJ and Dax were both nuts about her." Immediately he winced. "Of course that was a long time ago," he said with a sideways glance at Liz.

"You aren't hurting my feelings," Liz insisted, hoping she didn't sound defensive. "I think I knew he wasn't really serious about me." She took a sip of wine. "I don't hold a grudge."

The band kicked the music into high gear, playing a fast number that lured several couples onto the floor.

"Dax isn't such a bad guy," Mitch said, leaning closer. "He's just not ready to settle down yet." He speared a prawn with his fork. "DJ is the one I envy."

"Why is that?"

When Mitch didn't reply, Liz turned away. "Sorry, I didn't mean to pry."

He shook his head. "Going to a wedding makes a guy start thinking about settling down, I guess."

Liz could picture him with a big house, some kids and a dog. A sheepdog or a golden retriever. What she couldn't quite imagine— or just didn't want to—was a woman standing at his side.

"What about you?" he asked. "Do you want a family?"

"Sure, someday," she replied evasively. "I don't plan to get married for a long time. First I want to build a solid career."

A flash of something unreadable crossed his face before he bit into a prawn. Had she been too forthcoming? Maybe he'd expected to hear that nothing would *ever* come before work.

"All finished?" he asked.

Looking down, she was surprised to see that she had cleaned her plate without noticing.

"Yes, I am," she replied, wondering whether

she should elaborate on what she'd said. Before she could decide, he'd dumped their trash into a nearby container and returned with his hand extended.

"Dance?" he invited.

The band was playing another lively song and the floor was crowded with gyrating couples. She couldn't really picture Mitch letting go like that, but she was curious, so she stuck her hand into his. Perhaps she could loosen him up.

To her surprise, he fit right in, but before they could really warm up, the number ended. As the first notes of a familiar ballad whispered through the room, Mitch held out his arms.

A sudden feeling of expectation made Liz hesitate. She couldn't very well refuse and leave him standing alone, so she swallowed and stepped into his embrace. He gathered her close, tucking their clasped hands between them.

Following his lead was effortless, as though they'd done it a thousand times before. His heart beat steadily beneath her palm and his cheek rested lightly against her hair. Her eyes drifted shut. His warm breath tickled her skin as she floated, wrapped in music and warmth.

Someone bumped her and she staggered against him. Her eyes flew open as his arms tightened protectively.

She turned her head and looked directly at Russ Chilton, who was dancing with someone's grandmother. Without bothering to apologize, Russ turned away.

"You okay?" Mitch murmured.

She nodded. "It's getting awfully crowded."

"Let's take a break from all this," he said quietly. Without releasing her hand, he led her off the floor and through the knots of people.

"Pay no attention to Russ," he said after they'd gone through a door into an empty hallway. "He's been in a perpetual uproar about all the changes to the area."

They rounded a corner and Mitch stopped. "If Chilton had his way, Thunder Canyon would still be a tiny ranching community and the women would all be home having babies."

"And washing out their men's socks?" Liz teased. "How do you feel about that?"

Mitch rested his hand on the wall by her head. "This doesn't seem the time or the place for a philosophical discussion."

He was so close that she could have reached

up and kissed him. If he wasn't her boss...
she would have been strongly tempted. Of
course, if he kissed her, she wouldn't protest.
It might even be a good idea to get it behind
them so they could work together without her
wondering...

She could tell when a man wanted to kiss
her and Mitch showed all the signs as the
silence spun out between them. His eyes,
locked on hers, had darkened and his cheekbones were slightly flushed. Anticipation
made her breathless.

A door slammed and he straightened
abruptly, leaving her to wonder whether he
would have followed through or resisted
temptation. As voices sounded from down
the hall, he shoved his hands into the pockets of his slacks.

"Shall we go back inside?" he asked.

She couldn't very well disagree. With a
nod, she followed him back to the noise and
the crowd. As she sneaked glances at his
broad shoulders in his well-cut suit jacket,
she would have given a lot to know what he
was thinking.

"Would you like another drink?" he asked
with a nod toward the bar. "The line's gotten shorter."

"What I'd really like is to leave, if you don't mind," she said.

She had done what he asked by coming with him, but she didn't feel like socializing. Her only regret was not having the chance to slow dance with him again, but that probably wouldn't be a good idea. Not while she was so attuned to his nearness.

"Sure, no problem." His hand rested briefly on her back. "Let's say goodbye to DJ and Allaire first."

Despite her resolve, Liz was still a little unhappy when he didn't try to dissuade her from leaving.

Mitch was disappointed. He'd been thinking about asking her to dance again, but she had come with him as a favor, so he couldn't very well insist that they stay.

"Excuse me for a minute," she told him after they'd said goodbye to the happy couple. "Shall I meet you by the door?"

"I'll get our coats." He watched her work her way through the crowd with a mixture of pride and annoyance as masculine heads turned her way.

Not only was she beautiful, but she was good company. Overall, he hadn't felt so at ease with a woman in a very long time. Out in the hallway, he'd been tempted to steal a kiss, but he didn't want to rush her.

"Did you catch your date on the rebound?" Marshall asked from behind Mitch as he got his topcoat and her white wool. "You did notice that Dax is nowhere to be seen, didn't you?"

"She's over him, she told me." Mitch glanced at the people around them. "Where's your girlfriend?"

"You must mean my fiancée, Mia," Marshall corrected him, looking pleased.

Immediately Mitch stuck out his hand. "Congratulations, bro. I can't believe you're actually going to settle down."

"Me either." Marshall shook his head. "Won't our folks be surprised? I think they expected you to beat me to the altar, since you're the serious one and all that."

Mitch caught a glimpse of Liz by the door. "Don't write me off yet," he said, half to himself. "That's my intention."

Marshall turned, too. "So I was right all along—you do have the hots for her." He slapped Mitch on the back. "Way to go. Just make sure your brain keeps pace with your—"

"It's not like that," Mitch interrupted as he

waved to catch her attention. "She deserves a lot more than what someone like Dax could ever give her."

Liz waved back as she waited for him.

"And you think you're the one to give it to her?" Marshall asked. "Forget what I said. Don't rush into anything, okay?"

"So it's okay for you, but not for me?" Mitch asked, annoyed by Marshall's attitude. "And here I was going to ask how you'd feel about a double wedding."

For once, Marshall didn't have a snappy comeback as Mitch walked away with a grin. He'd tossed out his last comment just to annoy his know-it-all brother. But when he joined Liz and helped her on with her coat, he knew exactly what he wanted.

Just Liz.

Chapter Four

When Mitch pulled up in front of Cates International, Liz immediately unfastened her seat belt. "Thanks again," she said brightly as she opened her door. "No need for you to get cold."

Before he could react, she was out of the car. On the drive back from the reception, she'd already told herself to stop trying to figure out if he had really wanted to kiss her. It was *exactly* the kind of question that would have totally consumed the old Lizbeth in her quest to land a husband.

New Liz wasn't about to hang around and see what happened next. She'd taken control of her own life and she was setting her own rules. Besides, Mitch had said himself that his reason for inviting her tonight was so he wouldn't have to go alone.

"Liz?" His door swung open and the gravel crunched beneath his feet.

In her haste to unlock her Jeep, Liz dropped her keys. She and Mitch both bent down at the same time, nearly cracking heads as he beat her to the keys.

"Everything okay?" he asked, handing them back to her with an odd look. At least he wasn't into juvenile games like dangling them above her head.

"Of course." After she'd gotten her door open, she gave him another big smile. "Well, it's getting late and I have a lot to do tomorrow, so I'm going to run along."

A breeze sprang up, ruffling Mitch's hair as he stuck his hands into his coat pockets. He stared as though he was trying to figure her out.

"Would you like me to follow you home?" he asked.

Liz stiffened. "Why?" she blurted.

"I was offering to make sure you got home safely," he said calmly. "That's all I had in mind, honest."

"Oh." Despite the chill in the air, Liz's cheeks felt as though they were on fire. "I'm sorry," she mumbled, feeling like an idiot for overreacting. "It's really not necessary, but thanks."

At least now she wouldn't have to worry about him making moves on her. He probably couldn't wait to get away!

Mitch gripped the edge of her door and held it open, his face unreadable. "No problem. For the record, I'd never want to make you feel uncomfortable, so you've got nothing to worry about."

His words made her feel even worse. As he waited for her to get into the Jeep, she reached out to touch his sleeve.

"I should have known better," she said. "Would you like to come over for some coffee?"

The invitation was out before she realized she'd intended offering it. Now he'd think her indecisive as well as defensive.

His mouth quirked at the corners. "Is this some kind of test?" he asked. "Do I pass if I refuse?"

He was making fun of her. She bit her lip to keep from making things worse.

All around them it was silent and the road

was empty, yet she felt perfectly safe with him. Her instinct told her that he wasn't the kind of guy to take advantage. In fact, he would probably step up to protect her if she needed help.

"I'm not that complicated," she said in response to his question about a test. "It's just coffee, to show that I'm sorry for jumping to conclusions."

He reached out his free hand and traced his fingertip down her cheek. "Another time."

His refusal surprised her, and the light touch sent a shiver of reaction through her. She didn't want to apologize again and there seemed to be nothing else left to say. With a nod of agreement, she finally got into her car. He shut the door firmly and stepped back while she started the engine, waved one last time and drove off.

When she glanced in her mirror, he was still standing in the pool of light, a solitary, unmoving figure. She wondered if he ever got lonely. Fighting the sudden impulse to make a U-turn, she kept going.

When the taillights of Liz's Jeep finally disappeared around a bend, Mitch took a deep breath and willed his rigid muscles to relax.

Tipping back his head, he looked up at all the stars in the clear night sky.

Apparently he wasn't as good at hiding his feelings as he'd thought. He'd been telling the truth about offering to see her home safely, but he wouldn't have refused if she'd invited him inside. Beyond that, he hadn't allowed his imagination to wander.

He had watched her on many occasions while she tended bar; sidestepping invitations, ignoring propositions and coolly staring down those who weren't inclined to take no for an answer. Sure, she'd listened to their lines, laughed at their jokes, flirted enough to pump their egos. But as far as Mitch knew, she made a habit of leaving the bar alone when her shift was done.

Except for a few moments in that deserted hallway this evening when she had echoed his awareness of her, he doubted that she viewed him as more than an escort. That was something he fully intended to correct in due time.

Even a dedicated career woman needed an occasional break from the grind of work. If he had his way, she would be spending those breaks with him.

Before Mitch drove home, he checked his

cell for messages. It was no surprise that his brother had left him a text message.

2x wedding? R U nuts?

With a snort of laughter, Mitch stuck the phone back into his pocket. Let Marshall stew until morning.

When Liz entered the front door of the office on Monday morning, it was back to business as usual. She doubted that Mitch would ask her out again. Even though she had proven to herself that she was capable of spending time with a man without sizing him up as husband material, why push her luck? Like dark chocolate, Mitchell Cates was just too darned tempting.

Except for getting the third degree about the wedding from Kay Costner during lunch on Saturday, the rest of Liz's weekend had been filled with the usual chores and errands. She'd vacuumed and dusted the cabin, bought groceries and given herself a manicure.

Her sister, Emily, had called on Sunday, but Liz hadn't mentioned the wedding. Emily was like a herd dog, intent on taking care of everyone else. If she thought Liz was seeing someone, she wouldn't rest until she had extracted every bit of information.

To herself, Liz justified the omission as not being worth mentioning—despite the fact that attending with Mitch was *exactly* the kind of thing she would normally have confided in her big sister.

Before Liz had a chance to sit down, Mitch appeared in the doorway to his office. In his green "Cates International" knit shirt and slim jeans, he looked less like the boss and more like one of his own workers. But not, unfortunately, less attractive than he had in his suit on Friday evening.

"You aren't afraid of flying, are you?" he asked before she could greet him.

"Flying?" she echoed as he approached her desk. "No, why?"

"I've got a meeting tomorrow in Spokane," Mitch replied, idly rubbing his jaw with his fingertip. "You might as well come with me and meet the dealer, Harlan Kingman. He sells more farm equipment than anyone else in eastern Washington."

"Spokane?" Liz was starting to feel like a parrot, only capable of repeating key words. "How long will we be gone?"

"I'll have you back here before quitting time," he replied. "Harlan wants to show off his new showroom and take us to lunch. It wouldn't hurt for you to look up his Web site when you have a minute, too, Kingmantractors.com."

Mitch had told her before that there would be some traveling involved with her position as his assistant, but she was a little relieved that they weren't staying somewhere overnight. Before that happened, she needed to get her awareness of him as an attractive male under stricter control.

"Are there arrangements for the trip that I should make as part of my duties?" she asked. "Or anything else you need done?"

He'd already turned away. "No, thanks," he replied over his shoulder. "We'll leave from here at eight-thirty, so just don't oversleep."

Liz recalled his comment the next morning as she drove to work. Not only had she thoroughly checked out Harlan Kingman's business on the Internet, she had also read through his file. Combined with her previous study of the equipment sold by Cates International, Liz felt quite capable of dealing with anything that might come her way.

While she waited for Mitch to get off the phone and tell her it was time to go, she filed a stack of invoices for Nita. On her way back past Mitch's office, Liz poked her head through the open doorway.

"Morning," she said. "How are you?"

When he saw her, he smiled and pushed back his chair. Papers were scattered across his desk as though he'd been working for a while already.

"You look sharp," he said, eyeing her dark gray sweater and matching pin-striped slacks.

She wasn't sure how to interpret his comment. "Thank you," she murmured.

Mitch wore an open-necked dress shirt and black jeans. As she hovered in the doorway, he shrugged into a wool athletic-style jacket with leather sleeves in the company's familiar green and gold.

"I need to speak to Pete in the warehouse," he said, sliding his laptop into its case. "I'll meet you up front in five minutes." With a last look around, he followed Liz out the door, shutting it firmly behind him.

She took the time to visit the restroom, then donned her jacket and checked her tote to make sure she hadn't forgotten anything. Besides the usual contents, she had packed a paperback book, a water bottle, a legal pad and a nutrition bar as well as a company brochure to reread on the plane. She wanted Mitch to view her as diligent and eager to learn.

When they arrived at the airport a few minutes later, he parked his truck near one of the hangars that lined the landing strip. Liz knew that quite a few private planes came here, ferrying skiers to the nearby resort and eager newcomers to the town that had grown from a sleepy western attraction to a booming investment opportunity.

"Let's go see if the pilot is ready to leave." Mitch led the way to the tiny office connected to the hangar. Painted above the door in large blue letters was a sign reading Hansen Air Service.

Liz followed him silently, hoping their transportation wouldn't turn out to be a tiny plane with a single engine. After he took care of the paperwork, they went through another door into the huge hangar. Almost the entire far wall was open to reveal the runway beyond. Parked there was a sleek jet that resembled something a celebrity might own.

Liz half expected a flight attendant to appear at the top of the steps leading to the passenger cabin. "Wow," she muttered inadvertently when she got her first glimpse of the posh interior. "Is this yours?"

"No way." Mitch shrugged out of his jacket, then helped with hers. "I'm no John Travolta."

"If you were, you'd be flying it yourself," she replied, grinning. "Or disco dancing, I suppose."

He spread his hands with an exaggerated expression of regret. "No way. I'm not into white suits and anything I drive has to be firmly connected to the ground."

He glanced up when the door to the cockpit opened to reveal an attractive blonde wearing a uniform shirt and slacks. Her hair was cut very short, emphasizing her high cheekbones and long neck.

"Mitchell!" she exclaimed. "Welcome."

After they exchanged a brief hug, he introduced the two women. "Erin is an experienced pilot and I've flown with her before," he added. "You don't have a thing to worry about."

From the look Erin gave him, Liz wondered if he and the shapely blonde were more than acquaintances. Not that Liz cared, of course, whether or not they were.

"If you're ready, we've been approved by the tower for takeoff," Erin said.

Liz sank into the cushy leather seat Mitch

indicated and fastened her seat belt. Mitch took the seat facing hers and did the same.

"All set?" he asked.

She nodded as she took a deep breath. Her previous experience had been limited to larger planes, but she wasn't about to admit that she was nervous.

As if he could read her mind, he reached out to pat her hand. "Let's go," he told Erin through the intercom.

Mitch tried to keep his mind on business during the short flight, but with Liz seated close enough for him to inhale the fresh lemon scent of her shampoo with each breath, it was no small feat. Finally he set aside the paperwork he'd been reviewing with her.

"How do you like your job so far?" he asked, pouring each of them a glass of ice water from a pitcher in a holder.

Her big brown eyes shifted from his face to the writing pad where she'd been making notes. "I like it." She didn't sound entirely convincing, or perhaps she hadn't made up her mind yet.

Either way, how did he expect her to answer?

"And you're doing okay?" he prodded.

It probably wouldn't be wise to add that

he'd make whatever changes she wanted, just to keep her happy. She would probably walk if she ever suspected that he'd developed a crush on her.

After she'd taken a sip of water from the crystal tumbler, she looked at him with a resolute expression. "I'm learning a lot," she said firmly. "Thank you for bringing me with you today."

"You're welcome." In hiring Liz, he had certainly gotten more than he'd bargained for, he thought. He hid a rueful smile behind the rim of his glass as he drank the cool water.

How could he get the point across that getting involved with the boss wouldn't jeopardize her job? Quite the opposite, it would make the boss very, very happy. He would just have to play it by ear.

"You'll like Harlan," he said. "Just remember that he hasn't built up his business by being a cream puff. He likes to play the part of a good ol' boy who's struck dumb by a beautiful woman, but underneath he's as tough as nails, so don't be fooled."

"I'll remember," Liz replied, cheeks turning pink. She turned to look out the window as though suddenly fascinated by the view.

The plane must have hit a pocket of air because it made a sudden lurch, drawing a gasp from Liz.

When he glanced down at her hands, he saw that they were clasped tightly in her lap. At first he thought that referring to her as beautiful had embarrassed her, but then he reminded himself that she must get compliments all the time.

Apparently she wasn't as used to flying as she would like him to believe. Pretending not to have noticed, he, too, studied the clouds.

Had Mitch said she was beautiful? Liz knew she was blushing as she continued to stare out the window of the small jet, refusing to meet his gaze or to show how his offhand comment had affected her.

It was her brain she wanted him to admire, not her looks, she lectured herself silently and to no avail. Despite her resolutions, she *wanted* Mitchell Cates to find her attractive.

Was she doomed to remain a shallow, superficial flirt, ill-equipped to attain any goals that required more than a pretty face? Incapable of more than persuading some man to put a ring on her finger and love her?

Not that Liz thought less of anyone, male

or female, who wanted exactly that, but her aspirations had *changed*.

"Do you have a thing for cloud formations, or are you trying to bore a hole through the window and escape?" Mitch asked in a teasing voice.

Liz blinked. "Sorry. I was just thinking."

"About what?"

She scrambled for a reply. "The CC3," she blurted. "I wonder if we should offer it in more colors."

Mitch appeared perplexed. "Cows don't care about color," he drawled. "Besides, what's wrong with green?"

Liz shrugged. "Nothing. I'm just brainstorming."

He sat back in his seat with a slight smile on his face. It reminded her of his expression when they'd been together in that private alcove at the wedding. When she'd thought he might kiss her.

"You don't have to think about work all the time," he chided her gently. "Tell me what you like to do when you're not at the office."

The abrupt change of subject startled her. Was he just making idle conversation or was he genuinely interested?

"My life isn't very exciting," she replied.

"I like to read and to garden. I'm learning to knit and I've been working on a scarf for my brother, Eric, for Christmas. Someday when I have more time and more space, I want to start quilting."

Since his eyes didn't appear to be glazing over, she thought for a moment. "I enjoy cooking, but I'm not very good at it and it's not much fun to cook for one, anyway." Lord, was she as dull as she sounded?

"And I collect owls," she added with a sheepish grin. "That's about it."

Why hadn't she taken up skydiving or developed a passion for Aztec artifacts or glassblowing so she was *prepared* when someone asked?

His dark brows rose. "Owls?" he echoed. "Live or stuffed?"

Liz chuckled at the image of a row of stuffed owls lined up across her fireplace mantel.

"Figurines," she replied. "Ceramic, glass, carved wood, and I even have one made from marble."

"Ah," he said as understanding dawned. "I collect scale models of construction equipment."

"Like bulldozers and road graders?" she

asked doubtfully. Maybe she wasn't the only weird one on the plane.

It was Mitch's turn to chuckle. "That's exactly right. They're made of brass in perfect proportion and the detail is incredible. In fact, I just acquired an asphalt spreader from an online auction."

"Really?" She could think of nothing else to say except, perhaps, *why?* "That I'd like to see."

Mitch burst out laughing. "If you could look at your face," he exclaimed, shaking his head. "Owls and pavers, aren't we a pair?"

Apparently this was Liz's day to blush, because his comment sent fresh color to her cheeks.

"We'll be landing in about five minutes," announced Erin's voice through a speaker above their heads. "The temperature in Spokane is thirty-four degrees and clear."

Mitch was still grinning at Liz. "I guess you'll just have to see my collection to appreciate it."

"Is that anything like showing me your etchings?" she replied without thinking. Oh, God. *Now she was flirting with him!*

Something flared in his eyes for a moment

and then disappeared. "I guess we'll have to set something up and find out."

Mitch couldn't wait to get Liz away from Harlan Kingman and head for home. The entire time they'd spent at the dealership and then at Harlan's country club, Mitch had barely been able to resist demanding that the old coot back off.

Mitch had no idea whether Liz found Harlan fascinating for some reason Mitch couldn't begin to fathom or if she was merely playing a part in order to increase the size of Kingman's next order. The way she had spouted statistics about the Cates product line, talking up the benefits of the new model currently in production, had impressed even Mitch. Obviously she'd been studying in her spare time.

"It was wonderful to meet you," Liz told Harlan with a big smile as the three of them stood in front of the impressive new showroom with its two-story wall of glass. "I'm so impressed with everything you've built here."

"Why, thank you, Lizbeth," Harlan replied as she tugged her hand free of his big paw. "Y'all come back any time and see me." He glanced at Mitch. "And leave the boss at home next time."

"Don't hold your breath," Mitch replied, trying not to sound as grumpy as he felt. "Thanks for lunch." He stuck out his hand and Harlan pumped it enthusiastically.

"Thank *you*." Harlan gave him a broad wink. "I'll be talking to you."

Without another word, Mitch held open the passenger door to the rental car until Liz was settled inside. With a last wave, he slid behind the wheel and turned the key in the ignition.

Silently, he merged into traffic and headed for the airport. Beside him, Liz fiddled with a button on her coat.

"How do you think it went?" she finally asked in a small voice.

Mitch attempted to swallow his annoyance. It wasn't her fault that Harlan was an old flirt. Was Mitch any better, hiring Liz in order to get to know her better? Because he hadn't had the guts to just hit on her at the bar like other guys would?

"If I'm any judge of a situation," he said with a trace of sarcasm, "I think we can expect a bigger than normal order from Kingman next quarter."

"I guess taking the time to visit the customers really does pay off." She sounded pleased.

Mitch had to brake hard in order to keep from ramming a car that cut in front of him.

"Especially if the one doing the visiting looks like you." As soon as the words were out, he regretted them.

When he glanced at Liz and saw her frozen expression, he felt even worse. Before he could apologize, she swiveled to face him.

"What do you mean?" she demanded, voice tight. Two spots of color had bloomed on her cheeks.

"Nothing. I'm sorry." The vehicles in front of him had slowed abruptly or he would have reached out to pat her hand. As it was, he didn't dare take his eyes off the road.

"If Mr. Kingman was impressed with me, it was because I knew my facts, not because I... flirted with him, if that's what you're implying." Her voice shook. "He's a businessman."

Mitch took advantage of a red light up ahead to glance at her. "I said I was sorry."

Folding her arms across her chest, she flounced back in her seat, chin thrust out. She radiated disapproval like an air conditioner on high. Mitch nearly shivered from the icy blast.

His regret ratcheted up a notch. All she wanted was to be treated like a professional, but he'd blown it. Afraid of making it worse, he remained silent. Perhaps hiring her had been a mistake.

Chapter Five

Except for one or two necessary comments, the silence between Liz and Mitch lasted until after they'd boarded the jet again and left Spokane behind. This time Mitch had chosen a seat across the aisle from her. He'd immediately pulled down the table and spread out some papers from his briefcase.

Still upset, Liz stared at the page of a paperback she'd taken from her purse without comprehending a word. Her mind kept going in circles like a crazed hamster on an exercise wheel.

Had she made a big mistake in thinking she could reinvent herself? Perhaps she'd been right before and her only real talent was connected to her sometimes outrageous behavior and appearance. Maybe she'd set her sights too high when she had accepted the job with CI. If she failed, what did that leave her? Going back to bartending or finding a job as a clown at children's birthday parties? Either possibility sounded grim.

She glanced at Mitch, who was staring out the window at the darkness. All she could see was his blurred reflection in the glass.

If it was true that all she had to offer was her looks, then why had he hired her? She glared at the back of Mitch's dark head. To her consternation, he turned abruptly and caught her staring. Like a deer in some hunter's high beams, she froze, unable to look away.

Frowning, he finally swung aside the table and got to his feet. It was too late for her to bury her nose in her book, so she set it aside and folded her hands together as he reclaimed the seat across from her.

Defiantly she refused to avert her gaze as he raked his hand through his hair. His college ring caught the light. With his sleeves rolled up to reveal muscular forearms and a shadow of beard darkening his jawline, he reminded her less of an inventor slash engineer and more of a sexy magazine model. She suspected that under his business wardrobe he had the build for one. Even his questioning expression failed to mar the image.

Mitch cleared his throat, then leaned forward with his hands clasped loosely between his knees. His gaze was steady, yet unreadable.

"I shouldn't have said what I did," he began, voice low. "You didn't do a thing wrong. Actually, you amazed the hell out of me with all the stats you tossed out about our inventory. Despite his weasely attitude, I think Harlan was impressed, as well. When did you find the time to pack away so much information, anyway?"

"Whenever I didn't have something else to do, I would study the catalog," she replied, secretly pleased that he had called Kingman a weasel. She had dealt with way too many Kingmans when she tended bar.

"I took some of the brochures home, too," she added.

Mitch's mouth relaxed slightly as though he was going to smile, but then he refrained. "I'm awed by your initiative, but that's not what I wanted to discuss right now."

Liz braced herself. Despite his seeming approval, was he going to fire her? What would she do then, go crawling back to Grant? The thought of begging for her old job made her stomach churn.

"Look," Mitch continued, "I know what Harlan's like. He's a male chauvinist dinosaur, but his attitude isn't completely uncommon for someone his age. You handled him like a pro."

His exclamation loosened something in Liz that had been twisted into a tight knot since Harlan had almost refused to let go of her hand. Mitch was right; there would always be men who tried to treat her like an object. That didn't mean she had to allow it or to let their attitudes upset her. How professional was that?

"I know what you're trying to say," she replied, "and I appreciate it, but since you were obviously aware of Mr. Kingman's attitude and you admit that I did nothing wrong in how I treated him, then why were you so upset?"

Mitch studied her for a long moment, a muscle flexing in his cheek. "You really don't have any idea, do you?"

Confused, she shook her head.

"I guess I was a little jealous," he blurted,

just as they hit another air pocket. "I know I have absolutely no right to feel that way, but the way you seemed to hang on to his every word just got to me, I guess. Call it a guy thing, but part of me wanted your dazzling smile to be focused on me."

Liz didn't know what to say in response, or where to look. She wasn't sure if the bottom had fallen out of her stomach because of the sudden lurch of the plane or Mitch's abrupt confession. She wanted to tell him he had no reason to be jealous—especially of someone like Harlan—but Mitch was her boss, not her boyfriend. Perhaps he'd meant his comment as a joke.

He threw up his hands. "I can see that my grand admission has only made things more awkward, so it might be better if we both just forget I said that, okay? You made it clear that you take your future with CI seriously. I have every confidence that you'll be a great asset. In addition, I give you my word right now that you don't have to worry about me overreacting ever again."

"I…okay," she said, trying to inject some enthusiasm into her voice, even though she was more confused about him than ever. What did Mitchell Cates really want?

* * *

"Way to go, Hawks!" Marshall shouted, half rising from the couch in their folks' family room. "It's about damn time!"

The Seattle team had finally scored a touchdown against the Rams, grabbing the lead for the first time in the final moments of the nearly scoreless football game.

"Language," called their mom in a scolding tone from the adjacent kitchen.

Mitch and his brother exchanged knowing grins. "You can take a schoolmarm out of the classroom…" Mitch chanted in a low voice.

"I heard that!" she exclaimed, accompanied by a giggle that had to have come from Mia, who was helping her.

"Your mother's got hearing like a bat." Their dad lounged in a leather recliner that had been a Christmas gift from Mitch. Frank had a beer in one hand and a bowl of pretzels within reach on a side table.

"Heard that, too!" More feminine laughter floated over the noise from the television, a flat screen that Marshall had given them.

They didn't all get together every Sunday, but Mitch enjoyed the times they did, especially when his younger twin brothers could make it home from college, too. Despite their absence today, it was nice to be here. Their mom, Edie, was a great cook and their dad had mellowed considerably since "the Cates boys" had kept him on his toes with their endless antics and wild ways.

As the clock ran out on the game, Marshall got to his feet and stretched. "I guess I'll see if Mia would like to get some fresh air."

His casual tone and innocent expression didn't fool Mitch for a millisecond, but he resisted the urge to taunt his older brother, who had been known to threaten him with surgery without anesthesia.

"Ready for another beer, Dad?" Mitch asked their father instead.

He raised his half-full bottle. "No thanks, I'm good."

Mitch wasn't much of a drinker and he was driving home after dinner, so he decided against one, too.

"How's the job going?" he asked over the sounds of the postgame interviews. His father was a building contractor and all four boys had spent many a weekend and summer vacation working on various construction sites.

"If we can get the damned foundation

poured before the ground gets too cold, I'll be a happy man."

That'll be the day, Mitch thought, watching his father set his beer carefully on a coaster. Their father wasn't a "glass is half-full" kind of guy.

"Marshall told us that he's thinking about taking on a partner at the resort because he's been so busy," his dad added.

"He's a good doctor," Mitch replied evenly. "People like him."

A pause stretched awkwardly as a voice on TV raved about the wonders of frozen pizza.

"How's your business doing?" his dad asked belatedly.

"Good." He didn't bother to elaborate, never having felt that his career choice was as interesting as Marshall's.

Nothing beat having a son who was a doctor when it came to parental bragging rights. It was their mother who had pushed all four of the boys toward college, but Mitch often wondered how their father felt about none of his sons showing an interest in taking over his company someday.

"I heard you hired a bartender as your new secretary," his father said gruffly. "Can she type?"

"First of all, Liz worked in the Lounge at the resort, not just some bar," Mitch replied. "She's not my secretary, she's my assistant."

"I see," was all his dad said.

Mitch was concerned that his dad probably saw too much. Before Mitch could think of a way to divert his interest, his brother's voice sounded from the kitchen. His arm was anchored around Mia's waist and both their faces were red from the cold—or whatever they'd found to occupy their brief moment of privacy.

Mitch felt a painful jab of envy for what they shared. Mia was a sweet woman who obviously adored Marshall—and not just because he was a doctor.

"Do you want me to set the table?" Marshall asked their mother in an obvious bid for brownie points.

Predictably, he was shooed from the kitchen. As he sat back down on the couch, he sent Mitch a smug look. When they were growing up, the two of them had always competed with each other for their parents' attention—when they weren't getting into trouble.

"I was just asking your brother about that woman he hired," their father told Marshall.

Mitch tensed, hoping Marshall wouldn't repeat his comment about a double wedding, especially since Mitch hadn't returned Marshall's calls about it.

"You mean Lizbeth," Marshall replied. "I always thought she was wasting her talent behind the bar," Marshall continued. "Liz is a smart girl with great people skills. I can see why Mitch hired her."

Mitch slumped with relief. He should have known that his brother wouldn't rat him out to their father.

"I'll be sure to pass on your comment," he said. "She's doing a great job at CI so far."

He stiffened when Marshall winked. Uh-oh.

"Did Mitch tell you he took Liz to DJ Traub's wedding last weekend?" he asked their father with an innocent expression that was as fake as the ficus tree in the corner.

Their father's grizzled brows shot up as he looked from one son to the other. "Is that right?"

"Dinner's ready," their mother announced from the doorway. Holding a bowl of salad, she beamed her give-me-grandchildren laser straight at Mitch.

"You took *who* to a wedding?" she asked.

"Mitchell, are you seeing somebody? Anyone I would know?"

"Thanks a lot, bro," he muttered to Marshall, who'd already stood up.

"Anything that deflects the heat off Mia and me," Marshall retorted under his breath. "If you think it's bad now, just wait till you bring a girl home."

"What are you two whispering about?" their mother demanded, glancing suspiciously from one to the other.

"Nothing, Mom," they answered in the perfect unison of long practice as they headed for the dining room. Mitch and his elder brother might pick on each other, but they knew when to stand together against a common adversary as well.

Liz was pleased that Mitch asked her to help him with a presentation for a small convention in Billings. Since their trip to Spokane, his attitude toward her had changed. She told herself that it was because he was starting to see her more as a member of the team and less like an unproven new hire. At least she hoped that was the case.

"I don't normally attend such small conferences," he explained after Liz returned to his office with two cold cans of soda from the break room. "When I was just starting out, the folks who put this one on each year were very supportive. I landed my first order there."

It didn't surprise her that he would feel a sense of loyalty. She knew that from comments she'd heard from his other employees. He provided them with free healthcare and other generous benefits from the first day they started work.

"Billings is a lot less hectic than the big shows in Vegas and Colorado," he continued. "Compared to the hundreds of booths, long lines and no time for a deep breath, it's more like a mini-vacation, a chance to do a little work and catch up with old friends."

As she sipped her soda, Liz was glad of the excuse to watch the shifting expressions cross his face. She didn't have to sneak quick glances at the way his mobile mouth shaped different words or his eyes as they narrowed or lit up, or the sweep of his thick lashes when he blinked and his habit of lifting his brows when he asked a question. Now she could study his face openly, trying to absorb every word instead of just the sound of his voice, which was deep and rich. And just a little too distracting.

Today he wore snug jeans with scuffed western boots and a faded denim shirt that he'd left open at the neck. She had never been particularly enamored of the cowboy image, having seen too many wannabes with belt buckles the size of turkey platters, but the mental picture of Mitch in a Stetson working cattle from the back of a quarter horse had just become her number-one fantasy.

And she didn't even know if he rode, although she would be surprised if he didn't in this part of the country. She'd never run into him at the stable where she took the occasional lesson.

"I can see why you look forward to the trip," she ventured when it became obvious that he expected some kind of response. "It sounds like the best of both worlds."

"Selling isn't really my favorite part of the business," he confided. "At heart I'm an engineer, and most of the time I'd rather tinker in my shop, but I'm confident that you'll turn out to have a real talent for it. You connect with people."

Had he just hinted that she might take over sales someday? "I'd like that."

Setting aside her soda, Liz went back to proofreading the captions he'd written to accompany the photos in a new handout. Although Liz had never considered herself a real brain, she had a gift for grammar and punctuation, two subjects that Mitch claimed were a weakness of his.

"That's why I want you to go with me this time," he said as he stared at the computer screen. "It helps to know the people you're dealing with."

"Really?" She didn't know whether to be pleased or alarmed, but she knew from reading his itinerary that the conference ran over two days starting with a banquet on Thursday evening. "Will we fly again?"

He shook his head absently. "I like to drive. It only takes a couple of hours and the roads are still in pretty decent shape."

Silently she digested the idea of being confined in a car together with a lot less room than the private jet. They would also, she assumed, stay at the same hotel.

He'd told her there would be occasional travel with the job, but that had been before she had gotten to know him. Before she had realized that his more serious personality, black hair and golden brown eyes appealed to her. Mitchell Cates could be more of a threat to her well-being than any other man, if she wasn't careful.

"Earth to Liz!" His teasing voice penetrated her thoughts. "Can you stay a little late tonight, just for a couple of hours, and help me to finish this? I'll order us a pizza so we don't starve."

"No problem," she replied, pleased that he seemed to really listen whenever she ventured an opinion, even though she still had so much to learn.

He pulled a tattered menu from a local pizza delivery out of a drawer. "What do you like?"

"Everything except anchovies," she said, trying to keep her mind on the question and not the way he looked with his hair falling onto his forehead and the beginning of a beard shadow darkening his jaw. Coupled with his casual clothes, it was enough to make her seriously rethink her indifference to the cowboy mystique.

"I'm with you there," he said. "I'm not a fan of crunchy little fish."

It took a moment for her to recall the subject, and then she refused to succumb to his grin. Everyone else had gone home and the building was silent, making his office seem far more intimate than usual. Even the piped-in music had quit. When she did speak, she was almost tempted to whisper.

She phoned in their order and they went back to work while they waited. He had been teaching her to use a software program to deal with brochures and catalogs. Once they were done with the layout, he'd e-mail it out to the printer.

"What's wrong?" he asked as she sorted through the photos. "You're frowning."

Liz studied the shots of the portable calf-tipper, a smaller version of the basic unit which was mounted on a trailer for use during roundup.

"These pictures aren't very interesting," she said, dissatisfied. "They need something else with them to catch a person's eye and liven them up."

He sat back in his chair, folding his arms behind his head. "I suppose we could hire a few models in bikinis like some of the new car ads."

She gave him a withering look. "And women in swimwear would tie in with farm equipment just how?"

His smile brimmed with humor. "Guys like equipment and they like pretty girls, especially if they show a lot of tanned and toned skin. How much more of a connection do you need than that?"

She shook her head, trying with limited success to smother a chuckle. "Forget I mentioned it."

There was a loud knock on the front door.

"Pizza's here," he said, straightening. "We might as well eat at my desk. Would you get some drinks and paper plates while I pay the guy?"

Moments later neither made any attempt to hide their hunger as they sat side-by-side, devouring warm slices loaded with cheese and toppings.

"Why don't you put some of your employees in the photos?" she suggested, licking sauce from her finger. "You could mention their names and job titles, even show them working."

He took a large bite of his pizza and chewed it with a pensive expression while Liz held her breath.

"That's actually a pretty good idea," he said when she was beginning to wish she'd kept quiet. "And they probably work way cheaper than swimsuit models."

Resisting the urge to punch him in the

arm, she returned his smile. "My point exactly."

"Think you can handle it?" he asked. "Start by getting a photographer in to take some shots for me to look at."

Liz tried not to whoop with excitement. "I'll take care of it."

When they were finished eating, Mitch's cheek was smeared with sauce. Without thinking, she leaned toward him.

"Hold still." She gripped his chin with her fingers so she could dab at the spot with a napkin. No point in getting sauce all over the keyboard.

With a startled expression, he complied.

She didn't realize that she was licking her lips in concentration until she became aware that his attention had riveted to her mouth. His eyes had darkened and he was watching her intently.

In the tense silence, he lifted his gaze and sudden awareness crashed around her.

"What am I going to do with you?" he muttered, leaping to his feet.

Before she could ask what he meant, he leaned down to capture her hands and pull her up to face him. When he flattened her palms against his chest and held them there, she could feel the expanse of muscle under his shirt and the solid thud of his heart. She longed to burrow her fingers between the buttons and touch his skin.

"I want to kiss you." His voice was low and rough, his cheekbones flushed with color and his narrowed eyes were glittering down at her, black as obsidian.

Liz's pulse thudded like a drum. She slid her hands up and under his collar, curling her fingers in the soft fabric of his shirt as though to hang on for dear life in case her trembling legs were to give way. Anticipation hummed through her, making her feel as though she were poised at the top of a perilously high jump. Ready to take the plunge without even the aid of a bungee cord to break her fall.

A tiny frown pleated his forehead between the dark slash of his brows. "Liz?"

Was he waiting for her permission? Of course he was, she realized with a burst of understanding. He was her boss—he didn't want to take unfair advantage.

Without speaking, she leaned closer and slid her arms fully around his neck. Before she could urge him closer, he cradled her face gently in his hands, stroking her lower lip with his thumb.

Her last cohesive thought as he covered her mouth with his was that she hoped he didn't expect her to go back to writing copy for hydraulic cow tippers as soon as they were finished.

His lips brushed gently against hers, warm and smooth, before settling there. She melted against him, arms tightening, breasts pressed to his chest. Slowly his exploration became more urgent, warmth turning to heat as he deepened the kiss. She welcomed the touch of his tongue, caressing it with her own as desire flooded her senses.

He lifted his head, but only to change the angle of his kiss. She felt his arousal, impossible to hide when he held her so tightly. His caresses became hotter, more insistent and her responses less restrained.

She pushed lightly against his chest. His arms tightened and the beginning edges of apprehension trickled through her. They were alone and she had encouraged him. What if he didn't allow her to pull away?

Before concern could turn to alarm, his grip loosened. With a groan of reluctance she found perversely gratifying, he pressed a last relatively chaste kiss to her lips and then he lifted his head.

"I knew from the first time I saw you that you'd be able to twist my resolve into knots," he whispered thickly. "You go to my head like 80 proof."

Liz wasn't sure if that was a compliment or not. His heightened color and the relaxed curve of his mouth indicated a hunger that was not yet fully banked, but he let his arms drop to his sides. He must have realized that he'd crowded her against the edge of his desk, because he stepped back to give her more room.

With her feelings in turmoil, Liz needed a few moments to herself. "I've got to get something from my desk," she said hastily.

He made a sweeping gesture toward the half-open door and she rushed from the room. She kept going past the reception area and straight on to the women's lounge.

When she burst through the door, her reflection in the mirror was like a slap in the face. Her lips were swollen, her cheeks flushed and several strands of hair had worked loose from her topknot to brush against her neck. Her eyes had a knowing glint that no amount of shadow or liner could achieve.

Her professional veneer had been ruth-lessly stripped away, leaving only the flirtatious image she had tried so hard to eradicate or to at least disguise. Was this what had provoked Mitch into kissing her? Not an appreciation of her mind or the ideas she contributed or even her steadily increasing understanding of the business, but her subconscious come-hither smile? The availability she apparently still wore like a welcome sign, despite her best efforts?

She plopped down onto the burgundy suede love seat, overcome with a feeling of failure. Perhaps she should be thrilled that he wanted to kiss her, but what did it matter if he was attracted to her for all the wrong reasons?

Carefully avoiding her reflection, she got to her feet. She took a deep breath and left her sanctuary to confront her boss.

If he thought she was willing to provide a little distraction whenever he wanted a break, she had no choice but to set him straight.

Chapter Six

As soon as Liz fled from Mitch's office, he went to the window and stared out at the darkness, hardly noticing his own reflection in the glass. When he'd given in to the temptation that had been riding him for too long and kissed her, he hadn't thought about how she might take it.

What he should have done, he knew now, was to take her somewhere for dinner first—on a date—not make her feel as though getting mauled by her boss was part of her job description.

Had he mistaken reciprocated desire for an unwillingness to put her job in jeopardy? He raked both hands through his hair, swearing under his breath in self-disgust.

"Excuse me."

Liz's reappearance saved him from dwelling on his own humiliation. Slowly he turned to face her with his thumbs anchored firmly in his wide leather belt to ward off the temptation of reaching for her again.

How was it that every time he looked at her, he was struck anew by the beauty of her face? Even though she had obviously put on fresh lipstick and tucked away the stray curls brushing her neck, she hadn't managed to erase completely the telltale signs of a woman who had just been thoroughly kissed.

He cleared his suddenly tight throat. "About what happened—" he began.

At the same time, Liz advanced into his office with her purse clutched in one hand. "That can't happen again," she declared. "Not while I work for you."

Hearing one of his own concerns actually spoken aloud as a threat was enough to light the fuse of his temper.

"Do you think I'm some predator who would actually take advantage of an *employee?*" he demanded.

He felt as though someone else had taken

control of his mouth—and certainly his better judgment—making him say things he would regret instead of giving her the apology she deserved.

Liz's cheeks had turned fiery red and she looked stunned. "No, that's not what I think," she retorted. "I don't—" She shook her head. "I'm not going to sleep with you."

"Maybe you should wait to be asked," he drawled. "If that had been my intention, I would have bought you a better meal than pizza first!"

Her eyes widened, shimmering in the light with what looked suspiciously like tears. Oh, God. Now he'd made her cry! Before he could begin to babble out the words of contrition she deserved, she spun around and bolted.

For a moment all he could do was stand frozen in place and gape at the empty doorway. What the hell had just happened?

His dithering had given her enough of a head start to get to her Jeep as he reached the parking lot. He shouted her name, but she didn't stop. Frustrated, he watched her leave in a cloud of dust.

Liz cracked open her eyelids the next morning after spending a long, miserable night trying without success to forget the humiliating scene from the night before. She wanted to pull the covers over her head, but instead she sat up and swung her legs over the side of the bed. Her head ached, the light hurt her eyes, which were swollen from crying, and movement made her stomach pitch like a boat in a gale.

Groaning, she staggered into her tiny bathroom, part of her almost relieved that her nausea gave her a semilegitimate excuse to call in sick. There was no way she felt up to facing Mitch right now, not after their blowup of the evening before. She could only hope that a day would be enough to put it behind her and pretend that kissing him had been no big deal.

Certainly not the earth-shattering event to cause everything that had followed.

Her throat burned when she remembered the chill in his tone when he had suggested that she wait to be asked before she assumed that he wanted to have sex with her.

The memory made her face heat all over again. Had she misjudged him as he claimed? She pressed her fingertips to her throbbing temples. No! She shook her head, then groaned when the movement echoed in her stomach. No matter his intentions, he'd been as affected by their kiss as she, of that she was certain.

Sticking out her tongue at her reflection, she found a bottle of ibuprofen in the medicine cabinet and took a couple with some water. Then she padded back to the bedroom and looked at the clock. Praying that Nita would answer the phone and not Mitch, she called in to work.

Mitch looked up from the trade journal he had been flipping through between regular trips out front to see if Liz had arrived yet.

"Yes, Nita?" When he saw his bookkeeper hovering in the doorway, his surly tone reflected his mood as accurately as a voltmeter measured electric current.

If she noticed, she ignored it. "Liz called," she said. "She's got a flu bug and won't be in today."

Mitch felt as if all the air had suddenly been sucked from his lungs. "Is that all she said?"

Nita nodded. "She sounded tired, poor thing."

"Okay, thanks." After Nita left, he swiveled his chair around so he could look out the window at the mountains. He hadn't gotten much sleep, probably because his conscience had kept him awake. On the way to work, he had been tempted to stop at the flower shop, but he didn't want to do anything to stir up speculation among the rest of the employees. Or to make Liz more uncomfortable than she must be already.

The machinists, in particular, were a wild bunch and he'd overheard several of them try to flirt with Liz whenever they could find an excuse to come into the office. They wouldn't say anything to him directly despite the informal work atmosphere, but the idea that comments might be made behind her back was enough to ratchet his foul mood up by several degrees. He felt like grabbing a hammer and taking out his frustration on a piece of scrap metal.

Bringing Liz personal gifts at work was definitely out of the question.

At eleven a buddy of his called to see if he wanted to meet for lunch. Mitch was about to agree, hoping the distraction would improve his disposition, when he had a brainstorm.

"Sorry, Lee," he replied, glancing at his watch. "In fact, you caught me on my way out the door."

Agreeing to a rain check later in the week, Mitch ended the call, spirits lifting, and looked up a certain address. Without giving himself time to reconsider, he grabbed his jacket and hurried back to Nita's office.

"I'll be out for a couple of hours," he told her.

After quick stops at the drugstore and a deli he liked, he glanced at the directions he'd printed from the Internet and headed out of town.

When Liz woke back up halfway through the morning, her headache was gone and her eyes no longer felt as though she'd poured sand in them. She took a shower, bundled her hair into a careless ponytail fastened with a scrunchie and donned a faded lavender sweat suit she should have tossed out long ago.

Padding to the kitchen in her bunny slippers, she stared into her half-empty refrigerator without a shred of enthusiasm. Whether from nerves or a bug, her stomach still didn't feel great. Soup sounded good, but she'd run out and not restocked. Perhaps toast and tea would do.

The sound of a vehicle pulling up out front distracted her. It wouldn't be Kay or her sister; both thought she was at work. Curious, she went to the front window and peeked through the curtain.

Oh, no.

A loud knock at the door made her jump back, hand pressed to her heart. Had he come here to see if she was really sick? To fire her?

She glanced down at her sweats and smoothed back her hair as the knock sounded again. Her Jeep was out front, so he'd know she was home. Could she say later she'd been asleep and hadn't heard him?

She bit her lip, trying to think, as her phone rang. Flustered, she snatched up the receiver without thinking.

"Hello?"

"It's me," Mitch said. "I've brought chicken soup. I hear it works wonders on the flu."

"I'm not hungry." She sounded like a cranky child. "Thanks anyway," she added reluctantly.

"Liz, we need to talk." He knocked again. "Come on, let me in."

How could she face him, looking the way she did? Superficial or not, she needed the confidence that came with attractive makeup and a decent outfit.

"The soup's getting cold," he persisted.

Her stomach chose that moment to let out a

growl that would make a lion proud. "Could you just leave it on the step?" she asked hopefully.

"Not a chance." His voice had become husky. "I promise I'll behave. You know you want it."

She ended the call and yanked open the door. Mitch still held his cell phone in one hand and two plastic bags in the other. "Can I come in?" he asked, looking sheepish.

"Yeah, okay." Resigned, she stepped back and opened the door wider. At least the cabin was reasonably neat, even if she wasn't.

He stuck his phone back into his jacket pocket and was about to comply when a small panel truck pulled up next to his truck.

Liz peered past him. She wasn't expecting any deliveries. "Who—?" she muttered.

"Mind if I take these right into your kitchen?" Mitch asked. "I don't want the sherbet to melt."

"Sure." Distracted, she watched an older woman approach with a large bouquet swathed in green tissue and a clipboard.

"Lizbeth Stanton?" she asked.

When Liz nodded, the woman handed her an arrangement of roses. For a moment, Liz was too stunned to speak.

"Wait," she said as the woman went back down the steps. "Let me get my purse."

"All taken care of," she replied with a smile. "Enjoy."

Confused, Liz carried the bouquet inside. Who would send her flowers at this time of year? It wasn't her birthday.

Could it be that Dax had suffered a belated attack of conscience for breaking their engagement so abruptly? Ought she search the sky for flying pigs or assume that hell had finally frozen over despite signs of global warming?

When she set her prize on the kitchen table, Mitch was rooting around in the cupboards. "Got a pan for the soup?" he asked. "How do you manage without a microwave?"

"Check the drawer under the stove." She unpinned the card. "For the pan, not a microwave," she added absently.

He said something else, but she paid no attention, too busy reading the handwritten message.

Forgive me. Mitch.

Frowning, she turned to face him. He returned her stare with the saucepan in one hand.

Which was he sorry for, the things he'd said

or the kiss that preceded them? She reached down to touch one of the delicate blossoms. They were white and each petal was edged with pink.

"They're beautiful," she whispered, stroking one half-opened bud, "but they weren't necessary."

"I disagree." His voice was soft. Then he cleared his throat and busied himself with the soup. "The orange sherbet's in the freezer," he added in his normal voice. "It's good for a sore throat."

Feeling like a fraud, Liz pulled out a chair and collapsed into it. She watched as he transferred the soup from a plastic container and set the pan on a burner.

"Why are you here?" she asked.

"Bowls and spoons?" Apparently he didn't intend to answer her question.

She pointed mutely.

He set two places, humming under his breath. She remained at the table, looking at the roses instead of at him. A pink ribbon was wrapped around the vase and tied in a bow. Sprigs of white baby's breath contrasted with the dark green leaves. He stirred the soup, poured water into glasses and found some crackers.

After he'd served them both, he pulled out the chair opposite her and sat down. The bowl he'd set in front of her smelled too good to resist.

"Do you bring soup to all your sick employees?" she asked, holding her spoon with a hand that trembled.

His brow quirked. "What do *you* think?"

The first mouthful slid down her throat, but she barely tasted it. "Why did you come out here?" she persisted.

She had to know if she had somehow completely misread the situation last night. Had she overreacted to a casual pass, a mere testing of the water to see if she was willing? The debate had kept her awake most of the night and now she wanted answers.

He set down his soup spoon. "I came to make sure you're okay. Now finish your soup before it gets cold and then we'll talk."

She could see that he wasn't going to say anything more until she complied, so she emptied her bowl.

Getting up, he cleared the table over her protests. "No dishwasher either?" he asked.

"'Fraid not. The cabin might be primitive by your standards, but I wouldn't trade the setting for a penthouse in town." With the success of the ski resort, luxury condominiums were starting to appear, but she wouldn't have been tempted even if she could afford one.

"Doesn't it bother you to be so far away from your neighbors?" he asked as he ran water into the sink and added a squirt of soap. "Have you thought about getting a dog? A large attack dog with big teeth?"

She figured it was useless to protest his cleaning up, so she let it go. "I'd love a dog," she replied, debating whether to sneak into the bathroom and comb her hair. "But I didn't think it would be fair when I'm gone so much."

"I'll worry about you." He dried his hands and rinsed out the sink.

"It's not your concern," she said firmly as he resumed his seat across from her. "The cabin belongs to my sister and I've always loved it here."

"I didn't mean to put you into an awkward situation," he said abruptly. "I kissed you because I wanted to, but that doesn't mean that you couldn't push me away or tell me no, just because I happen to be your boss." An expression of distaste crossed his face. "God! I guess I should have explained all that before I ever touched you."

Despite the gravity of the subject, Liz found her mood lifting. "Or you could have handed me a disclaimer and maybe a release to sign," she suggested.

He leaned back in his chair with an affronted expression, but then his mouth relaxed into a reluctant grin. "So you can see why I didn't go through all that before I pounced."

"Who knew a simple kiss could get so complicated," she murmured, amazed once again at the magnetism of his smile.

"That's no excuse for the way I acted afterwards." Once again his expression had sobered. "All I can say is that I turned into a jackass. I was angry at myself, and I took it out on you and I'm sorry."

She stuck out her hand. "Apology accepted, and a lovely apology it was."

She wished she could add that she wanted him to be more than just her boss, but she didn't have the nerve. What if he didn't feel the same way? What if he decided that having an assistant with a crush on him wasn't worth the trouble?

He clasped her hand briefly in his. "Thank you." For an instant as he released it, he looked as though he might say something more, but then he pushed back his chair.

"Why don't you take a nap?" he suggested as he shrugged into his jacket. "If you're not better tomorrow, let me know if there's anything else I can do."

"I'm starting to feel better already." She followed him to the door. "It must be the soup." Or the flowers, or his company, she added silently.

He stopped on the step, hands in his pockets. "Well," he said briskly, "I'll see you later."

"Thanks again for everything," she said as he hurried away.

He waved without turning, so she shut the front door firmly. She stood at the front window and watched him back the truck around, but he didn't glance up. As he bounced back down the rutted driveway, she was relieved that she hadn't told him how she really felt.

Mitch cussed himself for being a coward all the way back to work. He'd gone to Liz's place with the intention of laying his cards on the table, but then he'd lost his nerve at the last minute.

Maybe it was better this way, he finally decided as he drove around to the loading dock to see if the shipment of assembly parts had arrived. No matter what else happened, she was proving to be a damned good employee. When the time came, he'd be sorry to lose her.

As long as he didn't give in to temptation again like he had last night and risk everything, just because being around her without touching her was almost more than he could stand. He'd better remember that he was damned lucky she hadn't walked out on him for good.

A semi truck was backed into the loading dock and he could hear the sounds of a forklift removing pallets of freight from the trailer. Even though his shipping clerk would be checking in the load, Mitch wanted to make sure it had all arrived and that nothing was on back order.

Thinking about Liz, looking adorable in her bunny slippers, with her face charmingly bare and her hair in tantalizing disarray, would have to wait until he had more time. One thing was for sure—he had no intentions of giving up.

"Mitch! I'm glad you're back," exclaimed the man who kept track of everything that arrived and left the warehouse, Pete Chambers. "We've got a problem with the shipment. One of the cartons of hydraulic subassemblies is missing."

He waved a handful of papers. Behind him, looking distinctly unhappy, stood the driver of the rig parked at the dock.

"I don't know anything about it," he protested. "The trailer was already loaded when I hooked up."

Mitch walked up to the two men and introduced himself to the driver, then shook his hand.

"Calvin Thoms," he replied with a twang in his voice. "Pleased to meet ya."

The hard miles were etched in his face beneath his soiled baseball cap. He reminded Mitch of a rodeo bull rider, bowlegged and slightly stooped in a western-cut shirt, worn jeans and tooled leather boots.

"We'll sort this out," Pete said. "The missing parts are listed on the bill of lading, so I've got a call in to the shipper."

Mitch knew they were crucial to the orders they hoped to fill before year's end. Before he could speak, Pete's cell rang.

He flipped it open and glanced at the screen. "It's them." He turned and walked away from the shop noise as he started speaking.

Mitch knew that Pete would handle the situation. Meanwhile, the truck driver wore an anxious expression as he shifted his weight from one foot to the other. He was probably calculating his losses if he ran out of hours and had to lay over.

Mitch clapped him on the shoulder. "Calvin, why don't you help yourself to a cup of coffee," he suggested. "You can wait in that room and Pete will find you as soon as he knows something."

"Much appreciated." His face finally relaxed into a slow grin. "Diesel runs the rig, but caffeine fuels the driver."

The next morning Liz returned to work. Except for asking if he'd sent the brochures to the printer, she did her best to follow Mitch's lead and act as though nothing had happened between them. It wasn't easy, but she managed.

He appeared more concerned about the arrival of some expedited shipment than anything else. As she made countless trips between her desk and his office, verifying information or asking questions, their proximity didn't seem to be a problem for him.

Liz was beginning to realize that pretending she didn't know what it was like to kiss him as though he was the only man on earth, to feel his strong arms holding her while hunger sizzled through her veins like the bubbles in champagne, was like trying to unring the proverbial bell.

Sometimes when he leaned over her desk to show her something on her computer monitor and she inhaled his clean, spicy scent, she felt light-headed. Or she caught a glimpse of awareness in his gaze before he blinked it away, a fleeting impression that he, too, found it difficult to pretend.

Only the knowledge that the inability to control her feelings would mean giving up a job she was growing to love was incentive enough to ignore those moments of silent communication. Of seemingly mutual longing.

Having convinced herself that lustful thoughts about him were stepping stones to disaster, she was stunned when he came out of his office the next morning and asked her to lunch.

"I've been craving a greasy burger," he said. "Why don't you come with me?"

As an offer, it couldn't have been more off-hand. Not like a dinner date.

"Sure," she replied just as casually. "I'm a sucker for greasy burgers."

"Good." Without another word, he walked away.

What had she expected, that he'd leap up

and click his heels together? Do a cartwheel? It was just lunch.

Just lunch turned into a habit. As they sat in the cab of his truck eating fish and chips on Friday, Liz suddenly realized he was staring at her.

"What?" she asked, angling her head so she could see herself in the rearview mirror. "Have I got tartar sauce on my nose?"

"Would you have dinner with me tomorrow night?" he asked. "Nothing fancy, just a Chinese place in old town that I heard was good."

The invitation sounded so offhand that it took her a moment to process.

"Unless you don't like Chinese," he added when she hesitated.

"No, I do," she exclaimed. "I just—"

"Have other plans?" he interrupted.

Did he know she hadn't dated anyone since Dax, unless you counted DJ's reception? Which Mitch had made plain *wasn't* a date.

"No," she amended. "I'd love to." After Saturday night, she promised herself, she'd climb back on the wagon. The Mitch-isn't-for-you wagon.

The Chinese restaurant was crowded and noisy. Liz noticed Mitch slip something to the

hostess, who found them a booth in a far corner behind a saltwater tank with coral chunks
and brightly colored fish.

Liz was glad she'd followed her instincts
and dressed casually. Under her silver parka,
she wore a green sweater and black pants, and
her favorite high-heeled black boots.

"Our secret's out," Mitch said after they
were seated with their menus. "Don't look
now, but we've been spotted."

Chapter Seven

Liz glanced around, but didn't immediately recognize anyone.

"I saw the receptionist from Marshall's office at a big table," Mitch said as he opened his menu. "Have you met her?"

"Yes, in his office one time," Liz replied. "Is it a problem?"

He patted her hand reassuringly. "Of course not. What about you?"

She knew that some people thought she'd dated just about every eligible bachelor in town, but she didn't care. People would think whatever they wanted, so why worry about it?

"Oh, yes," she teased. "I think you should crawl under the table."

He chuckled and then went back to his menu. They decided on a combo dinner for two. While they waited for their food, she watched the brightly colored fish.

"I had an aquarium when I was a kid," Mitch volunteered. "Mostly guppies and snails. How about you? Any pets?"

"A succession of shelter cats," she replied. "And my brother Eric had a turtle for a while."

The waitress brought them a pot of tea, which Liz poured into the delicate porcelain cups.

"I don't know anything about your family," Mitch said. "So you've got a brother as well as the sister who owns the cabin?"

"And another sister, Elaine. Emily's married and so is Eric. He's got two kids, so I'm an aunt."

The waitress came back carrying a huge tray covered with dishes. For the next few minutes, Liz and Mitch filled their plates and sampled everything. Mitch even fed her a bit of calamari, which she had never tried before.

"Mmm," she said. "Chewy, but not bad."

Neither had room left for dessert. Liz looked, but Marshall's receptionist was already gone when they left.

Liz kept up a steady stream of chatter on

the drive back to her cabin to cover up her nervousness. She still hadn't decided whether to invite him in, but she could have saved herself the trouble.

When Mitch walked her to the door, hand resting lightly on her back, he left the engine running. Given the price of fuel, it seemed like a pretty clear sign that he had no intention of sticking around.

"I had fun," he said when she turned to face him with her key in her hand.

"Yes," she agreed, flashing a smile. "Thanks for inviting me." Good heavens, anyone who overheard would think they hardly knew each other.

"Well, good night." She tried to read his expression in the glow of the porch light, wishing she knew what he might be thinking.

The wind blew a strand of her hair across her face and he brushed it away with his finger. "Liz…" he said almost reluctantly, leaning closer. "Ah, Liz."

She forgot to breathe, forgot to think as his gaze went to her mouth. He grasped her shoulders and she swayed toward him, eyes drifting shut.

His lips were cool on hers, but the kiss

heated quickly. And then, just as quickly, it was over and he released her.

"I'll see you on Monday," he said.

Blinking, she realized he was waiting for her to go inside. "Yes," she managed to reply without stammering.

She unlocked the door with fingers that trembled. After exchanging another round of good-nights, she slipped inside and shut the door behind her. Leaning against it, she listened as he drove away. She didn't move until she could no longer hear him.

On his way home from an informal game of basketball with a few other guys the next day, Mitch stopped at the store for groceries. He wasn't much of a cook, but he didn't like eating out all the time. At least, not unless Liz was seated across from him.

He hadn't planned to kiss her last night, he reminded himself as he pulled into a parking spot. He wondered if she realized that was exactly why he'd left the engine running, so that he wouldn't be tempted to stay. Then she had looked up at him with those big brown eyes and her full lips, begging to be kissed.

All his good intentions had turned to dust at her feet. He had wanted more than anything to press her up against the door, to kiss her breathless and then carry her inside. To make a feast of her and to ease the ache of desire that grew stronger with each day he spent around her.

Good thing he'd left the motor running or he might still be there with her rather than trying to burn off his excess energy by throwing a ball through a hoop. With a grunt of irritation, he exited the truck and went into the store.

When he spotted Russ in the frozen food aisle, Mitch was tempted to turn around and head in the other direction. As much as he had always liked Russ, he was growing weary of his friend's negative attitude and steady stream of pessimistic comments. However, before Mitch could make his escape, Russ looked up and saw him.

"Mitch!" he exclaimed with a rare smile. "How are you?"

"This is the last place I thought I'd run into you," Mitch replied, unable to resist a dig. "Isn't grocery shopping kind of domestic for a man's man like you?"

"Even a *man's man* has gotta eat," Russ retorted. "What's your excuse?"

"Likewise," Mitch replied, feeling slightly guilty for baiting his friend.

"From what I've been hearing, I would have figured you were eating all your meals *out* these days," Russ added with a challenge in his voice.

Mitch took a bag of frozen peas from the freezer case and tossed it into his cart. "What's that supposed to mean?"

From Russ's smirk, he knew he'd played right into Russ's hands. Mitch would have been better off to act as though the comment had sailed over his head and then made an excuse to get away as quickly as possible.

"A little bird told me you've been eating your meals with your new secretary," Russ taunted. "Does that include breakfast, too?"

Mitch's hands tightened on the handle of his cart. He couldn't decide which he would rather do, set Russ straight about his relationship with Liz or take a swing at him for believing the worst.

"I'm single, she's single," Mitch said instead. "I don't see that it's anyone else's business."

Russ's smug expression disappeared. "The problem, my friend," he said quietly, "is that all that girl wants is a ring on her finger. As long as the rock's big enough, I don't think she cares who gives it to her."

Mitch was normally slow to anger, but controlling his temper in the face of Russ's comments wasn't easy.

"Isn't it enough that she used to date your brother?" Russ continued relentlessly. "It's no secret that she nearly bagged Dax on the rebound from his brother getting engaged to his ex. And now Marshall's fallen for Mia, so you're about to make the same mistake as Dax."

"Don't tell me what I'm about to do," Mitch said through clenched teeth. "You don't know Liz. She's nothing like her reputation suggests."

Russ just rolled his eyes. "When you come to your senses, don't say I didn't try to warn you."

Mitch grabbed his arm. "Look, I appreciate your concern, but you're wrong about the situation and you're really wrong about Liz. I know what I'm doing."

"Having breakfast with her is one thing," Russ argued. "Just remember that you don't need to buy the cow—"

"Dammit, man," Mitch exclaimed, "watch what you say! I'm not scratching some damned itch here. I'm in love with her!"

As Mitch realized what he had just admitted, Russ merely stared, shaking his head. "Take it from me, pal, what you're feeling might start with a big letter *L,* but that doesn't mean it's love."

On the day of their scheduled departure for Billings, Liz left her overnight bag in her car. When it was time to leave, she set a box of brochures from the printer on her desk while she poked her head into Nita's office.

"I'll see you in a day or two," Liz said. "You've got my cell if anything comes up in the meantime."

Nita got to her feet. She had a fondness for Navaho jewelry and today she wore a silver necklace set with oval turquoise stones and matching earrings.

"Have a good time," she said. "Make Mitch take you to the steak house across from the hotel. Best beef in Montana."

Liz felt a totally irrational sense of disappointment. "Have you been to this conference?" she asked.

Nita shook her head. "I make my husband take me there for dinner every time we go to Billings."

"Thanks for the tip," Liz said, spirits lifting. "Bye."

As she went back down the hall, she heard Mitch's voice as he ended a phone call.

"Ready?" he asked, looking up when she hesitated in the doorway. Like her, he wore jeans with a green knit company shirt.

Now that departure was imminent, she felt a sudden attack of nerves. Being cooped up together in the cab of his truck for a couple of hours was bound to be stressful. She wished she could decide which would be worse, seeing that spark of interest in Mitch's gaze or its total absence.

"Sorry that we couldn't take the Lexus," Mitch said after they had pulled out of the parking lot. "The tipper's too heavy to pull behind it."

"Not a problem," Liz replied. They were towing a new model mounted on its own trailer. The unit had been polished until it glistened and now it was covered with a blue tarp to keep it from getting dirty.

"I see you got the memo," he said with a quick glance at her after they'd gone about a mile.

"Memo?" she echoed, determined to enjoy her first conference despite the undercurrents. "You mean the one about traveling light?"

She had managed to cram everything she

needed into one bag, a huge accomplishment
for her. Along with an outfit for tonight's
dinner and a swimsuit for just-in-case, she'd
packed clothes for tomorrow.

"Ah, but that was on page one," he retorted.
"I'm talking about the second page, the one
that dealt with travel clothes."

"You like?" She sat up straighter, preen-
ing. "Nita gave me a couple of her shirts that
she hadn't worn yet. I'll replace them when
my order arrives." She felt a sudden rush of
warmth when she noticed the direction of his
narrowed gaze.

"Nice," was all he murmured, but she saw
a muscle flex in his cheek. His hands tightened on the wheel.

She looked out the side window, staring at
the brilliant fall foliage. It was obvious that
he found her attractive, but what if that turned
out to be the only reason he'd hired her, not
because he genuinely thought she could do
the job?

It would mean that her looks really were
all she had to offer.

She clasped her hands tightly together
in her lap. Mitch wouldn't do that. He had
looked beyond the surface and recognized
her inner qualities.

"It's pretty country, isn't it?" he asked after a few minutes. "I never get tired of it."

The road wound through the picturesque mountain terrain in a gradual descent. Although there was already snow in the higher elevations, the pavement was bare and wet.

"I don't think I could live in a big city," Liz replied. "I'd feel crowded. What about you? Have you ever been tempted to move?" There must be challenges to running an international business from their little town.

Mitch chuckled. "One of the perks of being the boss is choosing the location. Besides, my family's here. The twins may choose to live somewhere else after they graduate, but Marshall's practice is growing and Dad's got more work than he can handle."

"Sounds like excellent job security for me," she said without thinking. "And the rest of your employees," she added hastily so he wouldn't think she was taking too much for granted.

"Most of them love living in Thunder Canyon as much as I do," he agreed. "With the resort operating year-round, I think people will keep moving to the area." He glanced in the side mirror at the trailer behind them. "Poor Russ hates to see it, but as long as development is controlled, I guess it's good business for the rest of us."

Liz wanted to ask if he planned to marry and settle down, but she didn't want him to think she was asking out of personal interest, so she remained silent.

"There are a bunch of CDs in the glove box," he said. "Why don't you pick out something to play?"

Curious about his taste in music, she took out a stack and looked through it. In addition to the country selections that were practically a requirement if you lived in Montana, there were a bunch of artists she didn't recognize.

"Who's this?" she asked, flipping one over to read the back cover.

"He plays acoustic guitar," Mitch explained. "Some of the others are cool jazz. I find that it calms me when I'm driving."

She doubted that he was the type to suffer from road rage, but one never knew. Perhaps there was turbulence or raging passion churning away beneath his surface calm.

What would he be like if he ever lost control? If he were overcome with desire, swept away by hunger to possess a woman he adored? The image made her shiver, but not with fear.

"The expression on your face makes me extremely curious as to what's going on in your head," he commented. "How about sharing?"

Flustered, she managed to drag up a cool smile. "Not on your life. A woman's entitled to a few secrets."

His probing gaze seemed to bore through her, but he had no choice but to return his attention to the road ahead. "Perhaps," he replied, "but that doesn't usually stop some poor helpless male from trying to discover them."

She had been around long enough to know when someone was flirting with her, and Mitch was definitely flirting. What she couldn't figure out was why. To kill time? Out of habit? Or because he was really attracted?

"I doubt you've ever been a 'poor helpless male' in your life," she observed.

He arched his brows. "You didn't know me back in junior high. Skinny, shy, a science nerd with a gift for blushing and stammering if there was a girl within a five-mile radius." He managed a pathetic expression. "It was pretty sad. Even you would have felt sorry for me."

"Even me?" she exclaimed. "Are you implying that I must have been hardhearted?"

"Trust me, I would have been scared to death of you in junior high. You were probably one of those girls who could crook her little finger and the male students would have a hormone surge strong enough to lift the roof off the building."

"Oh, you are so bad!" Liz had to laugh. "If you could have seen me with my knobby knees, flat chest—"

He'd glanced over at her. "No way!" he exclaimed.

Liz had no choice but to swat him. "I was your female equivalent. Shy, quiet, a skinny shadow who haunted the halls." She didn't bother to add that a year later she had blossomed, gaining curves that earned her sudden popularity that she exploited to the max. "What changed it for you?" she asked.

"Sports," he replied. "I discovered football at about the same time that I added some weight to my gangly frame. No one cared that I was a brain as long as I could throw a pass. You?"

"Boobs," she said with a grin. "No one cared that I couldn't throw a pass either."

She was gratified by his abrupt burst of laughter.

"Yep," he gasped. "No doubt about it. You would have terrified me."

Halfway to Billings, they stopped at a mini-mart at a wide spot in the road. Next to it was a rundown antique shop and another little building with "Closed" painted on the door.

"Time for a break," Mitch said, parking between two pickup-and-camper rigs that probably belonged to hunters. "Let's stretch our legs and get something to drink."

"Sounds good." When Liz climbed out of the truck, the air was cold and clear, so she slipped into her shiny silver parka that she'd tossed behind her seat. As usual, Mitch looked like a *GQ* model in a tan suede jacket that fit his broad shoulders perfectly. The man knew how to dress.

When she went up the front steps, a grizzled older man held open the door for her. When she thanked him, he tipped the bill of his bright orange cap. "Anytime."

Immediately, she felt Mitch's touch on her shoulder. "Coffee?" he asked, heading straight to the self-serve counter.

"I think I'll have a diet soda," she replied, stopping in front of the cooler.

When she met him at the register, he insisted on paying. "Anything else?" he asked, removing his wallet from his back pocket. "The dinner's not until seven."

"No thanks." She ignored the impulse to pretend they were on a different kind of trip, heading to a romantic weekend together. "I'll be outside." She needed some air before joining him back in the truck.

"Okay?" he asked a moment later, after they'd both removed their jackets and he'd set his coffee into the cup holder. "There are facilities behind the building if you need them."

She busied herself popping the top on her soda can. "No, that's okay. I'm good."

It didn't seem to Mitch that another whole hour had passed when they reached the outskirts of Billings. He drove through the hotel parking lot and pulled up under the covered portico in front of the main entrance.

"Want to check out the lobby while I get us registered?" he asked Liz. "We've got plenty of time to get settled before tonight's dinner."

"Good idea." Her smile was just as fresh as it had been back in Thunder Canyon.

Together, they went through the glass doors into the luxurious two-story lobby. The Western theme was accentuated by a life-sized horse and rider cast in bronze and displayed on a granite slab. Mitch knew from previous trips that the sculpture had been crafted by a well-known local artist.

As Liz wandered around, he proceeded to the front desk.

"Adjoining rooms?" asked the pretty young clerk after looking up their names.

With a wistful glance at Liz, he shook his head. Not this trip. "Something on the same floor will do."

"Certainly, sir." After she'd worked at the computer for a couple more minutes and run his credit card, she handed him two little envelopes containing the electronic keys to both rooms. "Rooms 303 and 314. Enjoy your stay."

He glanced around and spotted Liz studying a framed print of a cowboy carrying a saddle on his shoulder. From his free hand hung a bridle trimmed with silver.

Mitch allowed himself a moment to admire the way her snug blue jeans hugged her tempting female curves. The thought of slipping his hand around her narrow waist to pull her close fired him up like a teenage boy. If he wasn't careful, he might embarrass them both.

Lucky for him, he got himself back under control before she turned around. With a smile that made him breathless, she sauntered back over.

"This is quite a place," she said, looking up at the vaulted ceiling. "Did you know they have a spa? I might treat myself to a massage if there's time."

He opened his mouth and then shut it again without speaking. Was she *trying* to drive him crazy?

"But it's okay if there isn't," she added hastily. "I'm here to work, not have fun."

Was there a hidden message in her comment? He wished he understood women better. While his buddies had been gaining experience with the fairer sex, he had been hiding in his shop, building his business. Now that he'd found Liz, he thought as they waited for the elevator, he wanted to scoop her up and never let her go.

Filled with anticipation, Mitch stood in front of the door to Liz's room later that evening. He had warned her before they came that the dress code for the dinner ranged from good jeans and a clean shirt to suits and long dresses. It might be the only time all year that some of the women got to dress up. Tonight he wore a sport coat with his black jeans, but he hadn't bothered with a tie, or worse, the fancy leather bolo that some men favored.

Liz must have been hovering on the other side of the door, because she opened it the moment he knocked.

Tonight she'd left her hair long and straight. She was dressed in black, a sleeveless top and matching slacks with sexy flared legs.

"Come in," she invited. "Let me grab my bag."

Mitch stayed rooted in the doorway, ignoring his now familiar surge of reaction to her. Only when they were safely back in the corridor did he take a deep breath.

"You look spectacular," he said after he'd pressed the elevator button.

Although Liz thanked him, murmuring that he, too, looked nice, he got the impression that the compliment hadn't pleased her. Before he could ask if something was wrong, the elevator doors opened to reveal two couples he'd met before.

Amid a flurry of greetings, he and Liz boarded the car. They ended up walking to the banquet room in a group, so he didn't have time to speak with her privately.

Resisting the urge to curl his arm around her waist, he realized that it was time to scrap his original time frame. Normally a patient man, he couldn't wait much longer to find out whether Liz saw him as a boss—or something more.

After the other couples excused themselves, Liz entered the hotel dining room with Mitch. A bar had been set up in one corner. People stood with glasses in hand, talking and laughing. On the other side of the room, in front of a raised dais, were the cloth-covered tables. They were set with china, silver and sparkling glassware that reflected the light from a wrought-iron chandelier overhead. In the center of each was an arrangement of golden chrysanthemums.

"Let's get a drink," Mitch suggested, "and then I'd like to introduce you to some people."

By the time the dinner plates had been removed by the wait staff, Liz was almost totally at ease. She had met everyone at the large round table. In addition, a stream of people had stopped by to greet Mitch and he'd made a point to introduce her as his assistant.

Unlike the Traub wedding reception, where Liz had intercepted plenty of speculative glances, everyone here seemed interested in talking business and catching up. Mitch made a point to include her and she had actually been able to make a couple of intelligent comments.

After the dinner, the conference chair made a welcoming statement and introduced the rest of his staff. "Where did you learn so much about cattle roundups?" Mitch asked Liz as they joined the rest of the crowd headed for the exits. "Anyone would think you grew up on a ranch."

With his black hair and golden brown eyes, he was certainly one of the best looking men here. He gave no indication that he was aware of the sidelong glances he received from other women, but Liz noticed. She moved closer to him.

"I told you I've been studying," she replied. "I got a book about ranching from the library. Did you know that modern-day cowboys are more likely to ride ATVs and wear baseball caps to herd cattle than to do it on horseback wearing Stetsons? That's so sad!"

"That's progress," Mitch contradicted.

Even though her high-heeled sandals added a few inches to her height, he still topped her by a good few inches. "There's usually a pretty decent band playing in the lounge," he added. "Shall we stop by there and check it out?"

She hoped his suggestion meant that he didn't want the evening to end any more than she did. "Sounds like fun," she replied.

Surely he wouldn't have mentioned the band unless he planned on asking her to dance. Her pulse rate kicked up at the chance to feel his arms around her. It would no doubt make keeping her distance more difficult when they returned home, but it was a pleasure she didn't intend to forgo.

When they got to the dimly lit lounge, there were no empty tables. As they stood by the door, a stock breeder they'd met at dinner called out to Mitch.

"Come on over here," he invited from a nearby table. "We'll make room."

Mitch glanced down at her. "Okay if we sit with them?" Was it her imagination, or did he look disappointed, too?

She nodded and they joined the others. After greetings all around, Mitch gave the waitress their drink order.

"Dance?" he asked Liz.

His expression sent anticipation humming through her. "Yes, please."

He wrapped his hand around hers and led her to the crowded floor. Unlike the first time they'd danced together, he didn't bother with formalities. Instead, he pulled her into his arms, sighing when she nestled against him, and rested his cheek against her hair.

"I've been looking forward to doing this again for a long time," he whispered in a husky voice as his hand stroked her back.

As the notes wove a spell, Liz felt the basic rightness of being in his arms. And being at his side. Of being partners in every sense. Smiling, she rested her cheek against his chest and set her imagination free.

Chapter Eight

When the music finally faded away, Liz could have sworn she felt Mitch's lips against her temple before he lifted his head.

"I don't know about you," he said softly, gripping her hand, "but I'm finding this place to be way too crowded and too damned noisy."

As a pickup line, it wasn't the most original she had ever heard, but she didn't care. Mitch saw her as no one else had, giving her the freedom to truly be herself. Maybe someday she would know enough about the business to be a real partner to him in every way that counted.

Right now all she could think about was being alone in his arms. Nothing had ever felt so right.

"I'd have to agree," she replied with a slow smile. "There must be somewhere more quiet and—" daringly, she reached up and smoothed his lapel between her fingers "—more private."

His eyes narrowed, glinting dangerously. "I was hoping you'd see things my way."

Releasing her hand, he led her back to the table. The others were all talking, pitching their voices above the music so they could be heard.

Mitch handed Liz her drink and took a long swallow from his own before setting the glass back down. She sipped a little of her wine, but the warmth spreading through her had nothing to do with alcohol.

"Want to bring that with you?" he asked.

She shook her head. He scooped up his change, leaving a couple of bills for the waitress.

"See you all in the morning," he said easily.

Amid the chorus of replies, Liz left her glass on the table and walked out of the bar with him. Back in the lobby, away from the low lights and the music, she felt a distinct flutter of nerves.

Cupping her elbow with his hand, Mitch led her toward the closed and darkened gift shop. In front of the window, he once again took her hand, but this time he lifted it to his lips. Turning it over, he pressed a kiss to her palm and then he gently closed her fist, wrapping his hands around it.

Liz was helpless to look away from the intensity of his gaze. She couldn't have spoken if her life depended on it.

"There's nothing in the world that I want more right now than to be alone with you," he said quietly, still holding her hand in both of his. "Will you come upstairs with me?"

She searched his face, from the high forehead past the dark slash of brows to his heavily fringed eyes, such an unusual color of golden brown, and then down his straight, strong nose to his lips and his firm chin.

"Liz," he murmured, "you know you can tell me truthfully how you feel and I'll accept it, don't you?"

She bobbed her head. He had been truthful and she hated playing games. "I want the same thing you do," she whispered.

He drew in a sharp breath and his hands tightened their grip on her fist before he released her. His eyes blazed down into hers. "Come on," he urged, taking her arm.

Wasting no time, he went over to slap his free hand against the elevator button. Two women got into the car with them, talking about a nearby casino. Mitch and Liz rode without speaking.

The moment they got into his room, identical to hers in the light from a lamp he had left on by the bed, he locked the door behind them and pulled her into his arms.

"Liz," he said hoarsely, bending his head.

He kissed her with barely controlled passion. At the first touch of his mouth on hers, the dam of her reserve collapsed like a wall made of sand and she was swept up by a tidal wave of mutual passion.

Returning his kiss, she held nothing back. At some point, his stroking fingers found the zipper tab on her top and slid it downward. She barely noticed the fabric fall away, too busy with the buttons of his dress shirt.

"Pretty," he said, tracing the top edge of her black lace bra.

His feather-light touch against her sensitive skin sent shivers radiating through her. When she pushed back the edges of his shirt and leaned forward to press her open mouth against the satiny skin of his chest, he shuddered and his hands cupped her breasts. When he brushed her lace-covered nipples with his thumbs, heat burst inside her.

He freed her long enough to strip off his shirt, quickly followed by his shoes and socks. As she had suspected, his back and shoulders were beautifully formed.

She kicked off her sandals and let her slacks fall to the floor. As he watched, she stepped out of them. His gaze traveled from her face to her painted toenails and back again. Some men preferred reed-thin models to her curves, but he smiled with pleasure at the sight of her.

"You're perfect," he whispered, "but I knew you would be."

If she had thought he might be a controlled or methodical lover, she would have been wrong. After dealing with the rest of their clothing, he scooped her into his arms and kissed her deeply. Then, holding her over the bed, he let go, startling a tiny shriek out of her before she landed and he followed her down.

Wrapped in each other's arms, they rolled and tangled, explored, stroked and drove each other wild. By the time he stopped to sheath himself, she was trembling and aching with need.

"Hurry," she pleaded.

In the light from the bedside lamp she watched him as he came back to her.

"My lovely, lovely Lizbeth," he breathed, arms braced on either side of her.

She held out her arms. When he claimed her, there were no more words, no thought, just feelings as she held on tight. Soaring, she reached the peak and then held him as he followed, her name on his lips.

He wanted her to stay, but she knew if she did they'd get little sleep. Resisting his sales pitch, his kisses and his pleading, she dressed in her wrinkled clothes.

"You'll thank me tomorrow," she insisted.

When he saw that she couldn't be dissuaded, he pulled on his jeans and walked her barefoot down the hall to her room. At her door, he gave her a brief but scalding hot kiss.

"Can I come in?" he asked, looking hopeful.

Laughing softly, she shut the door in his face.

The next day, after a buffet breakfast, they went to the ballroom to get set up. The rest of the day was a blur of activity. Liz smiled and talked, shook hands and studied faces. She handed out brochures, business cards and free

pens. When Mitch was outside showing off
the calf-tipper, she manned the booth alone
and didn't do too badly.

They skipped the workshops and presen-
tations, but together they looked at the other
displays representing everything from tractors to hoof trimmers, DVDs on raising goats
to books on curing colic. Insurance agents
and financial advisors hawked their services.
Women sold hand-tooled halters and home-
made ice cream.

Between visitors, Liz tried to not think
about the night before or wonder what would
happen next. Mostly she failed.

Once Mitch came back with a steam-
ing latte for her, another time with a trio of
creamy yellow carnations that he pinned into
her upswept hair. For a brief moment, his big
warm hand rested possessively on the nape
of her neck and their gazes met.

"Breathtaking," he murmured, whether
about her or the flowers, she wasn't sure.
Dared not speculate.

They broke for lunch in the same room
as last night's dinner, sitting with a different
group at another big round table. During the
afternoon, each time she caught him watching her, she felt a fresh spark of pleasure. They

were a team now. She could see it in his face
when he looked at her, his gaze brimming with
approval and possessiveness.

Unbeknownst to Liz, Mitch had held on to
his room that morning while he checked her
out of hers. Sending her on an errand, he'd
left her bag there instead of taking it to his
truck.

Today had been one long endurance test
as he struggled to focus on work when all he
wanted to do was toss her over his shoulder
and head back upstairs.

He'd been right all along to think she was
perfect for him in every way. How long
should he wait before asking her to move in
with him? They could ride to work together,
bounce ideas off each other. Until they took
the next step, he didn't believe in hiding their
relationship, but neither would they flaunt it.
He knew she could make him happy in every
way and he fully intended to return the favor.
He could afford to indulge her and he would.

"I guess that's everything," Liz said after
Mitch finished securing the tarp onto the
calf-tipper. She peered through the tinted side

window of the extended cab, but she didn't see their bags.

"Are you sure you didn't forget anything when you checked us out?" she asked him. He had insisted on bringing everything down from their rooms while she went on ahead to the convention area.

With a quick glance around the deserted parking lot, he leaned forward to nibble on her lips.

"Who said I checked out?" he asked with a teasing smile. "Are you in such a big hurry to get home that you can't spare me a few private moments?"

She resisted the temptation to pull his head back down and show him how much she missed him already.

"I don't understand," she said instead. "What do you mean?"

He took his room key from his pocket and waved it in front of her. "Ever hear of late checkout?" he asked.

A fresh flush of desire stole through her body when she realized what he had done. "I suppose we've solved the mystery of the missing luggage," she said, trying to keep things light.

Mitch wrapped his arm around her shoulders. "How could it be missing when I knew where it was all the time?" he murmured as he led her through a side door back into the hotel.

They had the elevator to themselves, so he spent the brief ride tasting the sensitive skin below her earlobe. By the time they reached his room, she was burning up with need.

The first time they mated, they were still partly dressed. "Can't wait," he groaned, pulling her toward him.

"Yes, yes, please," she moaned as he filled her.

He shuddered, muscles rigid, then thrust again. Her world exploded and he groaned, a ragged sound, as he joined her.

"Wow," she muttered, boneless as he collapsed beside her. Never in her life had she given herself up to such raw, mind-blowing lust. "That was something."

"Yes," he gasped, rolling onto his back. "Next time...better."

Limp with satisfaction, Liz began to laugh weakly.

He struggled up onto one elbow. "What's so funny?"

She was sprawled across the bed, arms and legs flung out like a rag doll's. "Why do you hate me?"

"Hate you!" he exclaimed with an expression of horrified shock. "I'm so sorry! Did I hurt you?"

"Better, longer, trying to kill me," she wheezed with a big grin.

Mitch flopped back down, hand on his chest. "I hope you know you nearly stopped my heart with that comment, you shameless wench."

"Sure, call me names," she drawled.

After a few moments of compatible silence, Mitch sat up again and removed the shirt she'd only partially gotten unbuttoned before. He bent down to peel off his socks as she admired the width of his shoulders and the line of his back.

"You, too," he said, eyeing her with a meaningful glance.

She rolled over, groaning, still wearing her bra and CI knit shirt.

"Now there's a shot that would sell whatever we wanted," he mused.

"Fun-ny." While she took off the rest of her clothes, he pulled back the covers and laid her down.

With infinite patience, he made this time as much about romance as the last frenzied coupling had been about lust. When he finally slipped into her waiting heat, she knew without a doubt that she had found the other half of her self.

"Hungry?" he asked just as she was about to doze off, cuddled against his big warm body with her head resting on his shoulder and one leg thrown across his as though to anchor him close.

His question made her realize that she was starving. "I could eat," she murmured, torn between thoughts of food and staying where she was.

"Let's take a shower," he suggested, his voice a rumble beneath her ear. "Then we'll check out and I'll take you across the street for dinner before we leave town. Deal?"

The only better idea would be to stay in this room for the next month or so, but she didn't say it. "Deal," she agreed instead as she sat up and slid from under the covers.

"Too bad you can't stay like that," Mitch said approvingly. "I love looking at you."

She glanced over her shoulder in time to see him stand and stretch. "Back at ya," she murmured. Seeing him all decked out in one of his tailored suits back at work was going to be a little weird after this.

When he caught her staring, he looked her

boldly up and down. "Perhaps I'd better make my shower a cold one or we'll end up keeping the room for another night," he said. "Or another week."

Turning away from him was more difficult than Liz would have thought. What was she getting herself into?

Chapter Nine

As he worked on the computer in his private shop the next afternoon, fiddling with a new drafting program, Mitch was riding high. Sales were up over last quarter, production was running smoothly and his relationship with Liz was turning into more than he had dared to hope.

So far they seemed compatible in every way. The sex was great, her sense of humor made him laugh and her playfulness kept him guessing. He had every confidence that she would fit in well with his family once they got to know her.

He hummed tunelessly as he used the

mouse to highlight and drag a file from one folder to another. He looked forward to spending the holidays together, of perhaps tucking a very special gift under the tree with her name on the tag. He could picture his mother's smile at the prospect of two weddings to plan and two sets of grandchildren to spoil. Best of all, he could imagine Liz looking up at him with love in her eyes as she said *I do*.

When he thought about the shower the two of them had shared at the hotel, his body reacted as though it had been a month ago that he'd last been with her. In an effort to preserve his sanity, he turned his focus to dinner at the steak house, followed by the relaxing drive home.

The only thing that would have made the evening better would have been Liz spending the night, but she'd pleaded having too much to do. Today she'd been busy making final arrangements for the employee photo shoot and tonight she was meeting a girlfriend for dinner, so he had decided to stay late at work.

"Kay and I made plans a week ago," she'd said with a regretful expression when he stopped by her desk after a Chamber of Commerce lunch. "But I'll miss you."

He glanced at his watch and thought about

calling her cell, but resisted. Surely he could survive one night without her. Fourteen hours until she came to work in the morning, but who was counting?

Liz slipped into a chair across from Kay at The Rib Shack. "Sorry I'm late," Liz said. "I had to drop off some dry cleaning and there was a line."

"No problem," Kay replied with a cheerful grin. "I just got here myself." Coming to the resort for dinner tonight had been her idea.

Liz couldn't blame her friend for wanting to try Thunder Canyon's newest eatery. The reviews had been outstanding and Liz's brief engagement to the owner's brother was no reason to avoid it.

She glanced around, but she didn't see DJ. He and Allaire were probably still on their honeymoon.

For a moment, she and Kay both studied the menu in silence.

"Mmm, I'm going to have the baby back ribs," Kay said. "What about you?"

Liz closed her menu and laid it aside. "Half a barbecued chicken, fries and coleslaw. I didn't have time to pack a lunch last night and I'm starving!"

"How was the trip?" Kay asked. "From that new sparkle I can see in your eyes, I'd guess that you had a good time."

Liz wondered if Kay was telling the truth or merely bluffing. Liz had admitted to her before that she was attracted to her new boss, but didn't plan on doing anything about it. Normally the two women shared confidences, but Liz hadn't mentioned kissing Mitch and she certainly wasn't going to say anything about what happened in Billings.

"I learned so much at the conference," she replied enthusiastically. "I met people selling everything from bull semen to post hole diggers. Mitch knew just about everybody there, so it was fun."

A waitress approached to take their orders. Once she'd left again, Kay leaned across the table. "Did you sleep with him?"

"What?" Liz tried to appear shocked by the question, but she must have failed miserably.

"You did!" Kay crowed in a stage whisper, clapping her hands together soundlessly. "You shameless hussy, you slept with your boss!"

Quickly, Liz glanced around, but no one seated nearby was paying the slightest attention to them and the music would surely cover their conversation.

"I never said that!" she blustered.

Kay sat back, wearing a smug grin. "Oh, come on, girlfriend. This is me you're talking to. You haven't looked so happy in a long time."

While Kay took a sip of her water, Liz considered her last comment. Was she happy about the direction in which she and Mitch seemed to be headed? How could she not be, given her feelings for him?

"Tell me, what's he like?" Kay persisted. "It's always the quiet one who turns into a tiger in bed, or at least that's what I've heard." She batted her eyes. "Not that I've had any personal experience in that department," she added with a giggle.

"Of course not," Liz agreed. "And yes, he's way better than good," she couldn't resist adding. "But that's all I'm going to say on the subject." She couldn't imagine sharing the intimate details, even with her best friend. Some things were private.

Kay appeared disappointed. "Since I'm not seeing anyone right now, you could at least let me live vicariously through you."

"Not a chance," Liz said with a shake of

her head. "You'll just have to use your imagination."

"You're a meanie!" Kay made a face as the waitress brought their orders.

"Is there anything else I can get you?" she asked with a pleasant smile after she had set down their plates and drinks.

Both of them declined. "It smells wonderful," Liz said, mouth watering.

"Well, enjoy." With another big smile, the waitress left.

"So what happens next?" Kay asked as she buttered a slice of cornbread. "Will you be moving in with him? What's his house like? I bet it's really nice."

"I don't know and I haven't seen it," Liz replied, unfolding her napkin. "It's kind of complicated since we work together, but I'm not going to jump into anything and jeopardize my job at CI. I want to take it slow and see what happens."

Surely Mitch would give her some indication of how he wanted to handle their relationship around the office. Everything was different now, but today they'd hardly had a chance to talk at all. She'd hoped he might call tonight, but she'd turned off her phone during dinner. To take a call while she was with her friend would be rude.

After Mitch left a message on Liz's phone to call him when she got the chance, he went home and fixed himself a packaged dinner in the microwave.

Maybe he should get a dog, he thought as he sat down in front of the game with his feet propped on the coffee table. Perhaps he and Liz could pick out a puppy together later on when it wouldn't be left alone so much. He wondered what type she would like, a big outdoorsy breed or something smaller.

Restlessly he glanced at his watch. How long did it take two women to eat a meal and share some gossip? While he debated calling again, his phone rang. It was Liz.

"Hey, have a good time?" he asked after he'd muted the TV. He had already decided not to ask her over, since she had been reluctant to stay the night before and he had a full day of meetings tomorrow. The first time she saw his house, he wanted it to make a favorable impression.

"The food at The Rib Shack is really good," she replied. "Have you been yet?"

He felt a spurt of jealousy as he wondered

who she might have seen there. Dax? Some other former boyfriend?

"We had DJ's bachelor party at the Shack," he replied. "It's pretty nice, isn't it?"

"I got your message earlier," she said. "I had my phone off. Something going on at work?"

On the screen, the sports announcer's mouth moved silently. Mitch was slightly disappointed that business was the first thing Liz would think of, even though he'd placed it ahead of everything else for years.

"I just wanted to say that I miss you," he said, wishing she was with him so he could kiss her, hold her. He was looking forward to spending an entire night together so he could make love to her when they first woke in each other's arms. "I guess I'll see you in the morning."

"Miss you, too," she replied softly. "Good night."

He ended the call feeling vaguely dissatisfied, but not sure why. Perhaps it was because the call had felt a little awkward.

Despite the intimacy they'd shared in Billings, the progress they had made together, they didn't know each other very well in a lot of little ways. Personal wants and expectations. What did she wear to bed? Perhaps he would ask her at work tomorrow, just to watch the way her cheeks turned pink when she was flustered.

Pressing the mute button again, he tried to concentrate on the telecast with limited success as her image danced through his mind.

The next day at work, Liz was eating lunch at her desk when Mitch escorted his visitor, a sales rep from the phone company he'd been with for half the morning, out through the front doors. He had told Liz earlier that it was probably time for an upgrade and he wanted to find out what they offered.

She smiled up at him when he came back inside with his hair messy from the wind that had come up.

"What are you doing?" he demanded, frowning. "Aren't you going to lunch with me?"

His comment surprised her. Even though they usually ate together, she hadn't wanted to assume they would do so daily.

"I can do that." She put the lid back on her container of raw veggies. "I had no idea how long your meeting would run and I was getting hungry."

"Come on," he urged with an impatient glance at his watch. "I've got to be back by one."

She held her tongue, telling herself they would need to learn each other's ways, making excuses for him because he must have so much on his mind. During lunch at a local fast food place, she described the various ideas she'd come up with for the photo shoot.

"What do you think?" she asked, eager for his feedback.

"It all sounds fine to me," he replied.

Swallowing her disappointment, she nodded. "Okay, good." It was probably better that he didn't want to micromanage every step, that he had confidence in her to do a good job.

Before she knew it, it was time to go back to work. Neither spoke during the short trip back.

"Would you come over for dinner tonight?" he asked abruptly before they got out of his truck. "I don't cook a lot, but I've got a pan of Mom's lasagna in the freezer." His eyes darkened and he reached over to briefly squeeze her hand. "Besides, you haven't seen my house yet and I'm eager to show it to you."

Anticipation welled up inside her. "I'd like

that, too." She wanted to lean over and kiss him, but she knew that someone could walk around the corner of the building at any time, so she made do by returning the pressure on his hand before letting it go.

"Can I bring something, a salad or some wine?" she asked.

"I've got a bottle of White Zin on hand that should do nicely, but a salad would be terrific if it's not too much trouble." He waited for her to go ahead of him toward the office. "Seven o'clock?"

"I'll be there." Perhaps tonight they would make love again. The prospect made her feel slightly light-headed.

Right before he opened the front door, he leaned closer. "And don't forget clothes for tomorrow," he added softly. "You probably don't want to wear the same outfit twice in a row."

Despite her own feeling of anticipation, his casual assumption that she would spend the night with him left her feeling stunned. Swallowing hard, she managed to nod without meeting his gaze.

"Thanks for lunch," she murmured. "I've got to make some phone calls."

Without another word, he went to his office as she plopped down into her chair and stowed her purse in a desk drawer. She dialed Nita's extension to let the older woman know she was back, then turned on her computer and stared at the screen without seeing a thing.

Was she the one who was out of line for letting Mitch's attitude bother her? His casual assumption that they were a couple had thrilled her at first, but no one liked being taken for granted.

With mixed feelings, she waited for the afternoon to tick slowly past. Determined to keep an open mind, she left on the dot of five, stopping at the store for fresh lettuce and a cucumber.

"Lizbeth, is that you?" asked a friend of Emily's as Liz was about to get into line at the checkout counter.

"Fran!" She swallowed the impulse to glance at her watch. "How have you been?"

The other woman leaned against her shopping cart. "Have I seen you since John had surgery?" she asked.

Tempted to lie, Liz shook her head reluctantly.

"Well, I'll tell you," Fran said, "that was an ordeal for the entire family."

By the time Liz had heard all about his hospital stay, physical therapy and bout with their insurance company, the checkout line was even longer.

"Give John my best," she told Fran. "I need to get going."

"But what about you?" Fran asked with a quick glance at Liz's hand. "Didn't Emily tell me you got engaged?"

Liz waved her bare hand. "Old news."

"Oh, hon, I'm so sorry," the other woman said. "Well, John wants steak for dinner, so I'd better check out the meat case." She patted Liz's shoulder. "Don't worry," she said. "You'll meet someone else."

Liz didn't have the time to admit that she already had. "Thanks," she said with a brave smile. "See you."

Moments later, she pulled up in front of the cabin and hurried inside. After she had showered, smoothed lotion on her skin and dried her hair, she changed into jeans and a turtleneck. She hoped Mitch liked periwinkle blue, because her wispy bra and panties were the same delicate shade as her sweater.

Feeling attractive and desirable, she left her hair loose, adding silver earrings and fresh make-up. Dancing into her tiny kitchen, she washed the tomatoes that had been ripening on the counter, got down a large wooden bowl from the top shelf of the cupboard and went to work on the salad.

At a few minutes before seven, she set out for Mitch's house with the directions he'd given her earlier. As she drove down the dark road, the clouds that had filled the sky for most of the day finally delivered on their threat.

She refused to let the rain streaming over her windshield affect her mood. Within minutes she saw the street sign where she was supposed to make her first turn. It led her to a part of Thunder Canyon that she hadn't previously explored.

She wasn't surprised that Mitch lived in an upscale development tucked into the hills. The houses here were farther apart, set back from the winding road with lighted brick pillars, wrought iron gates or other elaborate entrances.

Just as the rain stopped, she spotted the granite boulder Mitch had described with his address chiseled into the face. Illuminated by a small spot, it marked his driveway.

Her hands tightened on the wheel and she took a deep breath. She couldn't see much of the grounds in the darkness, but her first glimpse of the house filled her with delight. With its steeply pitched roof and tall, glowing windows it reminded her a little of a ski lodge.

As she parked, Mitch came out the double front doors wearing jeans and a plaid shirt. His smile of welcome warmed her despite the chill in the air.

She climbed from the Jeep and he gave her a quick kiss. "Did you have any trouble?" he asked.

"Not at all." She handed him the bowl of salad, then got her purse and the dressing.

"Where's the rest?" he asked after she shut the door. "Didn't you bring a bag?"

She hadn't expected to be confronted about it in the driveway. "It's not that far back to my place," she replied, even though they both knew that wasn't exactly true. "I can't wait to see your house," she added brightly. "Did you have it built?"

To her relief, he took the hint and led her up the steps. "I bought it from someone who was transferred back east right after it was finished," he explained, holding open one of the carved wood doors. "My dad's in construction, so he looked it over for me."

They stopped in the two-story entry, where he set the salad bowl on a side table while he slipped off her coat and hung it up.

"This is beautiful," she exclaimed, turning in a slow circle.

The walls and vaulted ceiling were covered in wood that gleamed softly in the light from a chandelier. The fixture, made of irregular clear glass shapes, hung from a heavy chain. A staircase with a carved banister curved up the side wall to an open landing on the second floor.

Beyond the entry was the living room where two dark red leather couches faced each other in front of a rock fireplace. Brightly colored rugs were scattered over the polished wood floor.

"Let's postpone the tour until after we eat," Mitch said. He led the way to the dining room, where two place settings graced one end of the long table. He set down the salad bowl and Liz put the dressing next to it.

"Come on," he urged. "I'll show you the kitchen."

As they entered the luxurious room, the smell of the lasagna made Liz's mouth water.

"Your mother must be a wonderful cook," she said, inhaling deeply.

"For her it's a labor of love," he replied as he slipped on a mitt and opened the oven door. "I'll be sure to let her know you said that."

He removed the casserole and a roll of bread wrapped in foil. While he carried them to the table, she brought a bowl of croutons and one of grated parmesan.

"I think we're all set," he remarked after he'd gone back to the kitchen for a bottle of wine.

After he'd held her chair, he joined her. During the meal, she was able to relax and to put her reservations aside. When they were through eating, cleanup in his modern kitchen took only minutes.

"I can see why you thought my cabin was lacking in a few amenities," she teased him as she ran her fingertips over the polished granite countertop. "This is a cook's dream."

"It makes me happy that you like it." He closed the dishwasher door and pressed the control panel.

Liz cocked her head. "Is it running?" she asked. "I can't hear anything."

"It's super quiet," he replied, curving his arm around her shoulder. "Now, would you like to stay here discussing the appliances, or would you like to see the rest of the house?"

She slipped her arm around his waist and grinned up at him. "What do you think?"

He leaned down and planted a brief kiss on her lips. "What I think is that it's very important to me that you like this house."

The implication of his words along with the warmth of his expression made her spirits soar. This time when he kissed her, she met him halfway. He pulled her close, letting her taste the wine on his lips. When he finally let her go, she could barely catch her breath.

"I know it hasn't been very long," he said, hands on her shoulders, "but I can't help myself." He touched his forehead lightly to hers. "I love you, Liz," he whispered. "All I want is to make you happy."

She had never dared to hope that his feelings ran so deep. All she could do was to cling to him as happiness filled her, sweeping aside her earlier concerns.

"Oh, Mitch," she murmured, pressing her cheek against his shirt, "I love you, too."

For a few moments, they held each other tightly, neither speaking. This man, she realized, was everything she had ever wanted. He had looked beyond the surface and seen what no one else had. And he *loved* her, truly loved her.

"I'm the luckiest woman in the world," she exclaimed when he finally loosened his hold in order to smile down into her face.

"No," he corrected her firmly, tapping her nose with his fingertip. "I'm the lucky one." He appeared to really believe it. "Come on," he said. "Now it's doubly important that I show you around."

The rest of his house was just a blur to Liz. No wonder he had wanted her to stay with him tonight and now she wished she had brought a bag, after all. She could hardly stand the idea of leaving him.

The tour ended with his master bedroom. Impressed with its size and the decadence of the adjoining bath, she expected him to keep her there, but instead he led her back downstairs, holding her hand.

"Would you like another glass of wine or some coffee?" he asked. "I thought I'd put on some music and we could enjoy the fire for a little while."

He could have suggested they wash his socks in the spa tub and she would have agreed. Watching him light the fire, she had to put the breaks on her thoughts by reminding herself that their feelings were too new for them to rush into anything. Just knowing that he loved her was enough—more than enough—for now.

"I'd like some more wine," she murmured, stroking his chest possessively. Loving the idea that she had the right to touch him, kiss him. Knowing from the glitter in his eyes that she affected him as strongly as he did her.

He lifted her hand and pressed his lips to it. "You've made me so happy," he said. "Why don't you sit down and I'll be right back."

"Oh, I need to show you the list of employees for the photo shoot tomorrow." She'd almost forgotten. "I'll get my purse. It's in the dining room."

"I think we've got more important things to discuss tonight than work." With a smile, Mitch disappeared.

Liz retrieved the list from her bag. She didn't want to make a big deal and spoil the mood, but the shop foreman had told her to ask Mitch about one of the machinists she wanted to use for a model.

She unfolded her list and sat back down on the couch while he poured their wine. "It won't take long," she promised.

He set their glasses on the table in front of the couch. "You're determined to talk business, aren't you?" he said, looking slightly annoyed. "When I hired you, I had no idea what a workaholic you'd become."

"Don't say I didn't warn you," she cajoled. "I told you I wanted a career."

He sat down next to her, his gaze roaming her face. "And I've been pleasantly surprised at the great job you're doing," he murmured as he took both hands in his.

"Surprised?" she echoed, her smile faltering. "What do you mean? That you didn't think I'd be able to do it?" She searched his face. "Why did you offer me the position in the first place?"

"Now, don't get upset," he cautioned her. "Everything is working out better than I'd hoped."

Despite the fire, Liz felt a sudden chill. She was tempted to take his statement at face value, to drop the subject entirely and talk about whatever it was *he* wanted to discuss. He hadn't answered her question, though, and she realized that she really, really needed to know.

"Tell me," she insisted quietly, her hands tightening on his, "what it was about me that made you first approach me? Was it my people skills, as you so charmingly put it, or something else?"

He glanced away, taking a deep breath, and the chill inside her began to spread, to grow colder.

"I'm embarrassed to admit it, but I suppose it would be better to clear the air," he said with a shrug. "I wanted to get to know you better, but every time I tried to talk to you at the bar, either you'd get busy or I'd, uh, forget what I wanted to say."

Liz struggled to focus on feeling pleased that he had been attracted to her. He had always seemed so quiet, so reserved.

"I first noticed you when you were seeing Marshall," he added. "When I heard about him and Mia, I was happy for them, but I was also happy because it meant he was no longer seeing you."

She remembered thinking that Mitch was nice and even better-looking than his brother, but all he seemed to care about was work. "But that was before Dax," she realized aloud.

Mitch looked uncomfortable. "Exactly."

Liz shook her head. She wanted to snatch her hands free and press them over her ears, but he must have thought she meant that she still didn't get it.

"I had to do something drastic, to get you away from the Lounge, before you met some other guy on the rebound from Traub," he explained. "The best way for me to get to know you better—and quickly—would be to hire you myself."

Chapter Ten

Mitch's explanation made Liz feel as though her heart had turned to a block of ice.

"Don't be upset," he coaxed as a shiver went through her. "Like I already told you, everything has worked out really well. You're doing a great job." He let go of her hand so he could run his fingertips down her cheek. "The important thing is how we feel," he added. "Right?"

She fixed her gaze on his earnest face. What did it matter why he had first been attracted to her? He knew now she was more than just a pretty face. Guys were visual creatures, right? It wasn't his fault; it was centuries of evolution that were to blame. *Playboy* magazine, MTV and she wasn't sure what else.

"You're right," she replied, forcing a smile. "I'm *very glad* we got to know each other."

He let out a gusty sigh. "Wow," he said, "I'm sure glad we got past that. Maybe someday it will be an amusing story of how you and I first met."

"And how I got started at CI," she added. "Maybe when I'm vice president of the company."

He laughed even though she wasn't exactly joking. It was possible, wasn't it? If she worked hard and learned as much as she could?

"Trust me, in a few years you'll barely remember that you worked there." He picked up their wine glasses and handed one to Liz. "Let's drink to the future."

Numbly she held onto the stem of her glass. "I thought we were going to be a team, to work together."

"That's certainly one way of putting it." Smiling warmly, he clinked his glass against hers. "To us," he said. "Teammates."

Reality sank in. It hadn't been a business career he had offered her because he had never figured she was smart enough to handle it.

"Not at CI," she said aloud, her voice flat. As flat as she felt inside once her previous elation had all drained away.

He didn't know her, not really, and what was worse, he didn't want to, because he saw just what he wanted to see.

A pretty package with nothing of value inside.

"What?" he asked, looking genuinely puzzled. "You didn't really picture yourself spending the rest of your life working at CI as my assistant, did you?"

"Something like that." She set her glass back down. "I have to go."

"No, wait." He put his hand on her arm. "We're getting ahead of ourselves, but you certainly have a job at Cates International for as long as you want, okay? And when the time comes to…to reevaluate the situation, we'll both think about all the options and we'll discuss them."

She shook off his hand and got to her feet. "I have to go."

He shot up to stand in front of her, barring her way. "Now what's wrong? What do you want me to say, Liz? I thought we'd worked it all out for now."

"I've got a busy day tomorrow," she said

without quite meeting his gaze. "Thanks for dinner. Maybe someday I'll get your mom's lasagna recipe."

"Maybe we need to slow things down," he practically sputtered. "I think you misunderstood everything I said."

"You're right," she said. "Let's slow it down, way down. We should probably concentrate totally on work so I can show you what a fantastic job I can do."

She hadn't intended on breaking it off with him, but now that the words were out, she saw that it was the only way. She had to know in her heart that she kept her job because she was a valuable employee, not because she was sleeping with the boss.

"I don't understand," he exclaimed. "I thought you wanted me as much as I want you."

He lifted his hand as though to touch her face, but she pulled away. "So you're saying that I can't work at CI unless I keep sleeping with you?" she asked softly, clutching her purse as though it were a lifeline. "Is that the deal?"

He looked shocked. "We can't go back to just working together."

She ignored the pain twisting inside her

like razor wire, couldn't believe she had been so blind. "Then I'll have no choice but to give my resignation."

He threw up his arms. "Come on, Liz," he coaxed. "You aren't going to quit. You love your job."

But not as much as I love you, she thought. "You're right," she said, pulling the folded paper back out of her purse. "We'd both go crazy if I kept working for you." She shoved the list at him.

Automatically, he took it. "What's this for?" he asked.

She was determined not to cry, not until later. "The photographer will be there at ten o'clock in the morning."

"Why are you telling me?" he demanded.

She ignored the tiny voice of reason in her head, trying desperately to get her attention. "I'm sorry that I can't give you any notice," she said, fighting to keep her voice steady. "Under the circumstances, I don't think it would be a good idea." She drew in a deep breath. "I quit."

Without another glance at Mitch, she fled. Grabbing her coat without bothering to put it on, she dug her keys from the pocket and rushed out the front door.

While they had been too caught up with each other to notice, the rain had begun again and it was falling harder than before. It soaked Liz before she could get to the Jeep, mingling with the tears running down her face.

As she backed around in order to leave, she glanced up at the house she had fallen in love with on sight. A lone figure was silhouetted at the front window.

For one aching moment, her foot hovered above the brake pedal as every cell in her body urged her to go back. Maybe, if he came to the door, rushed down the steps…but the figure at the window didn't move.

With a sob, Liz pressed her foot down on the accelerator and drove out of his life.

"Come back," Mitch muttered under his breath, willing the brake lights to go on, for her to change her mind. Instead he watched the Jeep go down the driveway and disappear into the rainy night.

"Dammit, just come back and let me explain," he muttered.

Wandering back to the family room, he sat down in front of the fire and drained his wine glass. He debated tossing it into the fireplace to reduce his frustration. Since the set had been a housewarming gift from Grant, he restrained himself.

Instead he stared at Liz's half-full glass. With a shrug, he picked it up. When he saw the faint smudge on the edge, he put his lips where hers had been and drank it, too.

When he got to his feet, he noticed the paper she had left behind. She had been so excited about the project that Mitch couldn't believe she wouldn't show up for the actual shoot in the morning after she'd had a chance to calm down.

He never should have pushed her as he had, never should have admitted his main intention in hiring her. Hell, hadn't he told her what a great job she was doing?

He thought she would be pleased, even flattered. Instead she'd blown up like one of the firecrackers she reminded him of. Sparks flying in every direction, lots of drama. Even, he suspected, a few tears on her way home.

So why did she have to get so worked up, blaming him for something he couldn't control, falling for her so hard that he'd actually created a position for her in his company. Most women would be flattered! Too damn bad for him that Liz Stanton wasn't most women.

Apparently the woman her brother had told him wanted to get married more than anything else didn't want to marry Mitch. Or wish to have anything more to do with him.

By the time Liz got back to the cabin, the ache in her chest hadn't begun to ease up, but it had been joined by a feeling of panic.

Not only had she walked out on the man she loved, but she had also tossed her job back in his face—the same job she just happened to need in order to pay her bills. What had she been thinking?

For a moment she rested her forehead against the steering wheel, listening to the rain beat down on the roof of her Jeep. Then, feeling as though she'd been beaten from head to foot, she grabbed her purse and coat, took a deep breath and dashed up the front steps.

Wet and chilled, she got the door unlocked and hurried inside. Her teeth were chattering. She needed a shower and a hot cup of tea. Then she had to sit down and figure out what to do.

One thing was for sure, asking Mitch for her job back was out of the question.

* * *

After she'd stood in the shower until she quit shivering and the hot water was beginning to run out, she donned the ultimate comfort outfit: flannel pajamas, her rattiest robe and her fuzzy slippers. She made a cup of tea, got a cookie from the jar painted to look like a bumblebee and thought about calling Emily.

Her older sister had always been like a second mother to Liz. Emily wouldn't just tell Liz what she wanted to hear, as Kay might do. She would pull no punches and Liz needed to know whether her thinking was totally screwed up or if she was right to be furious with Mitch.

Of course the first thing Emily would do would be to give Liz an earful for quitting another job, probably the best one she'd ever had, and then she would scold Liz for getting in so deep with Mitch so quickly. Emily thought she'd already changed jobs too many times and she hadn't bothered to hide her opinion of Liz's engagement to Dax.

Liz winced at the memory of Emily's reaction. Maybe she wouldn't call her after all. She added honey to her tea and stirred it while she brooded.

No matter whether Emily was exasperated with her, she desperately needed to talk to someone who knew her, flaws and all. Even though it seemed like days since she had first driven to Mitch's house, so full of anticipation for the evening ahead, it was still probably early enough to call Emily. Even if Liz woke her up, she wouldn't complain. She was one of those rare people who loved being needed, and Liz needed her now.

By nine o'clock the next morning, Mitch had to face the fact that he had seriously underestimated Lizbeth Stanton. Apparently she'd been dead serious when she told him she was quitting.

A few minutes ago, he had snapped at Nita, dressed as a rather discreet belly dancer for Halloween, when she had offered to call and find out if Liz was all right. Now he had no choice but to admit the truth and ask her to have the temp agency send someone out right away. Before he faced Nita again, he looked through Liz's desk and found the photographer's card, then punched in the man's number.

If Mitch had to explain to one more costumed employee that he'd forgotten what day it was, he would scream.

"Just send me the bill for your time," Mitch told the photographer's assistant after canceling the shoot. "Perhaps we can schedule something in the future, but I'll have to let you know."

Right now, taking pictures of farm equipment seemed pretty damned unimportant compared to everything else that was happening.

After he ended the call, he looked up to see Nita standing in his office doorway with her arms folded across her chiffon-swathed chest.

"What's going on around here?" she demanded, rows of tiny gold bells on her veil tinkling when she moved.

Resigned, he motioned for her to come in. "Shut the door behind you, Delilah."

"Has something happened to Liz?" she asked as she sat down across from him and rearranged her colorful skirts, accompanied by more tinkling bells. She had known Mitch for too long for either of them to stand on ceremony.

He scrubbed his hand over his face. Several cups of coffee hadn't completely offset a sleepless night. His mind felt like thick, slug-gish glue.

"I guess you could say that," he replied dryly. "She came to my house for dinner last night."

"Ah," Nita said with a knowing expression. "So I was right."

"If you guessed that I'm crazy about her, you'd be correct," he retorted. "Not that it's done me any good."

"Why the self-pity?" she asked sharply, fancy gold earrings swaying. "It's not like you."

He touched his finger to a tiny donkey carved from petrified wood that she'd given him right after his first tipper had gone into production. *Stubborn,* she'd said at the time. *Like you.*

"We had an argument. She wanted to break it off, so I called her bluff and she quit."

"Quit her job?" Nita exclaimed.

"Yeah. Her job, me, everything." He could hardly believe he was having this conversation with a woman who was outfitted like Sa-lome, but he knew he could trust Nita to keep her mouth shut. She might be painfully blunt with him, but she was also extremely loyal.

"What did you do?" she asked.

Nita's assumption that it had to be his fault might have pissed him off if he hadn't felt so glum.

"I told her the truth," he said. "That was my first mistake." Quickly he gave Nita the ex-purgated version, starting with trying to talk to Liz at the bar and getting nowhere. By the time he finished describing their argument at his house, Nita was already shaking her head.

"What I can't understand is how men have managed to run the world for thousands of years without annihilating the entire human race," she drawled, the stack of bangles on her arm jangling with each gesture. "How can you all be so damned dumb?"

"I suppose that's a rhetorical question," he replied, his tone echoing her sarcasm. "Just how is insulting my ancestors supposed to help?"

She got to her feet, pacing to the closed door and back in her jeweled sandals. "You're intelligent enough to run this company, but you're clueless when it comes to understand-ing a woman you claim to love."

"I do love her!" he protested. "But no, I don't get how her mind works."

He must have appeared as pitiful and confused as he felt, because she stopped pacing and sat back down.

"Mitch, honey," she said, "put yourself in her place. Think about how *you'd* feel if she confessed that she'd been initially attracted to you because she heard that you're rich and successful, even though she knew nothing else about you." She paused for effect.

He nodded impatiently. "Go on."

"Now try to wrap your small male mind around the idea of being a pretty girl with a good brain." She shook her finger at him like a schoolteacher. "Only no one cares if you're smart. What matters is how you look." She raised her eyebrows. "You with me so far?"

He could see where she was heading. "Yes."

"So the prince comes along," she continued. "He seems to notice that you're an intelligent woman. That you have other qualities besides shiny hair or long legs. It's your *brain* that fascinates him and everything is rosy in the kingdom."

Mitch was beginning to feel sick. "But then he admits that he's just like everyone else," he said, taking over. "He loves your pretty face, but he could care less about the fact that you're sweet and smart and funny..."

"I think you've got the picture." Nita stood up again, dusting off her hands. "My work here is done." She sauntered to the door, hips swaying, and pulled it open. "The next step is yours."

With a last flutter of chiffon, she left.

"It's not that simple," Mitch muttered to the door she had shut firmly behind her. He was only just beginning to realize how much he must have hurt Liz with his selfishness.

Liz stared at her reflection in the mirror on the back of her bedroom door without one shred of enthusiasm. Her sister had been right the night before when Liz had poured out her heart.

"Since you aren't independently wealthy, the first thing you need is another job," Emily had told her firmly. "After you've found something, then you can afford to sit around and brood about Mitch, not before."

Emily wasn't being unsympathetic, just practical. She'd bailed out Liz in the past and Liz knew she'd be there again, but Liz was a big girl now and Emily was right.

All day Liz had hoped Mitch might call, even if it was merely to ask a question about work, but the phone didn't ring. This morning, after staring at her meager bank balance, she had made a few calls of her own.

The accounting firm where she used to work wasn't hiring and neither were three other former employers. That left her with two options, going to see Grant Clifton or hitting the streets with her résumé.

She had already called to make sure he would be at his office. Now she wrapped another strand of glittery ribbon around her ponytail so the ends dangled, then turned her head to study the effect. Even dressed in a plain black sweater and figure-hugging black stretch pants instead of one of the sexy outfits and heavy makeup she used to wear, she looked pretty good. Besides, it was her bartending experience that mattered, not looking like a hottie.

Leaning closer to the mirror, she added big hoop earrings, another coat of mascara and a final application of lip gloss. She blew her expression a kiss. If image was everything, she looked decent enough to pass inspection.

"Trust me," Mitch growled, "I'm in no mood for a party." He wished to hell he hadn't answered the phone when Marshall called, or let it slip that he and Liz had broken up.

All he wanted to do was to go home and sit in front of the fire with a half bottle of good scotch and get pleasantly sloshed.

"I won't take no for an answer," Marshall replied. "All the profits go to the hospital fund to help patients who can't pay. You promised you'd be here and every cover charge counts."

"How much does it cost?" Mitch demanded. "I'll send you a damned check."

Marshall chuckled. "Wouldn't be the same, bro. I expect you to bid big at the silent auction. If you're not here in an hour—in costume—I'll come and get you myself."

Before Mitch could tell Marshall what to do with himself, Dr. Charm ended the call. Maybe he was right and Mitch needed to get out for a couple of hours instead of sitting home and drinking alone. At least if he wore a mask, no one could see 'stupid' written on his forehead.

Resigned, he went to his walk-in closet to see what kind of costume he could come up with.

"Why do you want to come back to work at the Lounge?" Grant Clifton demanded as Liz sat across his desk from him. "Isn't Mitch paying you enough?"

When she first knocked on the door to Grant's office, he'd seemed pleased to see her. He'd even asked if she was going up to the lodge for the hospital benefit there. It was only when she broached the subject of getting her old job back that his smile had faded.

"I don't work at Cates International anymore," she admitted now, clasping her hands together tightly in her lap to avoid fidgeting.

Grant's eyes widened with disbelief. "No," he exclaimed, shaking his head. "I don't believe for a minute that Mitch would let you go. He's crazy about you." Immediately Grant clamped his mouth shut as though he'd let something slip. "At least that's what I heard," he muttered hastily.

"Actually, he didn't let me go. I quit," Liz admitted quietly. "Right after we broke up." She knew Grant would find out sooner or later.

With a sudden scowl, he leaned back in his chair and stared at her. "So what is Mitch now," he asked, voice dripping with sarcasm, "just another notch on your bedpost? Who's next, Liz? Will it be Russ Chilton? One of Mitch's younger brothers? Is there a single man in town you haven't dated or chased?"

His voice had gradually risen until he almost shouted the last couple of words.

Liz sat frozen in shock. "That's not fair." Her voice quivered and she swallowed hastily. "You make me sound like some kind of heartbreaker, but if you remember right, Dax broke up with *me!*"

Grant waved his hand in a dismissive gesture. "True enough, but I've seen how Mitch looked at you when he came into the Lounge. How could you leave a good man like him in the lurch?"

"It's a long story," she replied, "and not one I feel like discussing. All I want right now is to come back to work. I need a job."

"Because you walked out on a good friend of mine?" Grant retorted. "So I should hire you so you can break someone else's heart? I don't think so!"

His words were so unfair, his expression so judgmental that tears sprang to her eyes. "If you change your mind—"

"Believe me, honey," Grant interrupted, "as long as I'm in charge, there's no job for you at this resort." His gaze swept over her. "Are we done? I've got work to do." Opening a folder lying on his desk, he proceeded to study it as though she wasn't there.

Gritting her teeth to keep back the sobs of humiliation rising in her throat, Liz slid back her chair and got to her feet. She felt like a complete fool for coming here, for assuming she could get her old job back without a problem. Obviously she couldn't have been more wrong.

Maybe she should have dug one of her old revealing outfits out of her closet after all. Without it and a ton of heavy makeup, she wasn't even good enough to tend bar.

The only good part of this whole humiliating episode was that the desk outside Grant's office sat empty, so Liz was able to duck across the hall to the restroom without being seen. She had learned the hard way that there were no secrets in this town, so she was determined to escape without starting any new rumors.

After she'd sat in a stall long enough to regain her control, she risked a look in the big mirror. Her face was a mess, eyes swollen, nose red and cheeks pale as death except for the dark streaks of mascara that obviously wasn't waterproof, after all. It took her a few minutes to repair the damage well enough to make her escape.

When she slipped silently back into the

empty hall, the first thing she heard was Grant's raised voice coming through the open door of his office.

"How can you stand there and defend her after what she did?" he demanded. "I'd think you'd be grateful that I ran her off, not chewing me out!"

Despite her anxiety to get away undetected, Liz hesitated with her back pressed against the wall. It sounded as though he was talking to someone about *her*.

"You'd be lucky to have her back! She's the best bartender you've ever had."

She recognized Mitch's voice instantly and a wave of longing threatened to destroy her shaky composure. Then she realized what he'd said. Despite what she'd done, he was defending her!

"Good-looking women are a dime a dozen," Grant replied in a sneering tone. "Buddy, you need to understand that Liz Stanton isn't anything special."

"That's where you're wrong, *buddy.* My mistake was in not realizing until it was too late that Liz is a hell of a lot more than just another beautiful woman. She's smart, funny and she's damned hardworking."

There was a moment of silence, during which Liz wished she could see Mitch's face.

"Not only did I lose the best assistant I could ever have," he continued more quietly, so she had to strain in order to hear him, "but I'm afraid, as melodramatic as it might sound, that I lost my soul mate, too."

A door opened down the hall and a girl appeared. Liz had no choice but to leave before she was caught eavesdropping.

When she got back to her Jeep, she sat behind the wheel without starting the engine as she thought about what she had overheard. She replayed Mitch's comments in her head until she was more confused than ever.

Why did it matter so much to her that he'd been initially attracted by her appearance? Wasn't that exactly what she had first noticed about him, way before he'd offered her the job at CI? Before she got to know him at work and fell head over heels in love?

If the situation had been reversed, mightn't she even have created an opportunity to spend more time with him? Was it Mitch's fault that she'd always felt judged by her looks?

Was it any reason to deny them both a chance to find happiness together? All of a sudden the argument last night that had ended with her childish I'm-going-to-hold-my-breath-until-I'm-blue tantrum made no sense at all.

Desperately, she scanned the well-lit parking lot, searching for any sign of Mitch or his car. Since she had only heard his voice, she had no idea whether he was wearing a costume, but even if he planned to attend the party, he would probably drive up the hill to the main lodge.

Even though she waited for nearly a half hour, he never showed. Somehow she had missed him.

She went up to the lodge herself, driving slowly through the parking lot, but she didn't spot either the Lexus or Mitch's pickup truck. Refusing to accept defeat, she then went by his house.

She had no way of knowing whether both vehicles were parked in the four-car garage, but not a single light shone from the house. Just to be safe, she rang the bell, but there was no response. Perhaps he was at the lodge after all.

Nibbling her lip, she debated what to do next. She didn't want to call his cell, but if she didn't talk to him tonight, she might chicken out.

With a fresh burst of determination, she drove back down the hill toward town. Before she left Mitch's neighborhood, she passed a group of trick or treaters. Seeing the little ghost in the white sheet, the princess and the witch in a black pointed hat, Liz wondered if she and Mitch would ever have the chance to walk their children from house to house, as these parents were doing.

If she had anything to say about it, they would.

Disappointment flooded her when she finally got to CI and saw the empty lot, the darkened offices. With no idea what to do next, she decided to circle around the back of the warehouse before leaving, even though it was obvious that everyone was gone.

As the last of the adrenaline Mitch had been riding on since his confrontation with Grant finally drained away, leaving him exhausted, he shut off the forklift he'd been using to move the freight around.

All he had accomplished was to make a mess for one of the men to clean up in the morning. Before he had left the resort, he'd called Marshall and made his excuses over his brother's protests, but going home to walk through the empty rooms and picture Liz there was more than he'd been able to contemplate. Instead he had come here, to find some solace in the place he had created. To wear himself out so he could go home and crash without being haunted by questions that had no answers.

At the sound of the back door shutting, followed by footsteps crossing the empty warehouse, he walked from behind a stack of pallets and froze in his tracks.

He blinked hard to clear his vision, but he still saw the image of Liz walking toward him in the glow of the overhead light.

"Mitch?" she called out. "Can we talk?"

Oh, great. Apparently his vision came equipped with audio.

He knew he couldn't avoid her totally in a town this small, but he wasn't ready to see her. Not yet.

She stopped when there were still several feet separating them. He couldn't help but notice that her face, although as pretty as ever, looked strained.

"How are you?" He stuck his hands into his pockets to stop himself from reaching for her.

She shrugged. "Okay. You?"

"I talked to Grant," he said. "He told me what happened." He cleared his throat. "I'm sorry."

For a moment, she didn't speak as he wondered desperately what she was thinking.

"I was there," she said softly. "I heard what you said."

"You heard me?" he echoed. "I didn't see you."

She bit her lip, as though coming to a decision of some kind. "I was standing in the hall outside Grant's office." She took a few more steps toward him. "I acted like an idiot," she said, voice trembling. "You were right and I was wrong. I should have been flattered at the lengths you went to for my sake. Can you ever forgive me?"

"You want your job back?" he asked hoarsely. God in heaven, what was he going to do if she said yes?

She took another step, bringing her close enough for him to reach out and touch her. "I want the whole package," she replied, gazing up at him with her big brown eyes full of something he hadn't dared hope he would see there again.

Love.

He slipped his hands from his pockets,

but forced himself to keep his arms at his sides. "And what's in the package?" he asked, heart thudding in his chest like a flat tire on a trailer.

Gaze never wavering, she reached out to touch his arm. "Partners," she said. "In whatever capacity the two of us decide, whether it's boss and assistant or…whatever."

Her smile gave him courage. It was time to lay it on the line, to hold nothing back. He captured her hand in his before she could pull it away. Slowly he sank down onto one knee on the concrete floor.

"Wh-what are you doing?" she gasped, her fingers clinging tightly to his. "You don't have to—"

"I want you to marry me," he said, never more sure of anything than he was right now. "I'll buy you the biggest rock we can find if you'll just say yes. You can put on the fanciest wedding this town has ever seen, spend as much as you want, have a hundred bridesmaids, if that makes you happy."

Her expression was unreadable, so he barreled on, desperate to convince her. "I'll wear a pink tux if you want me to. Whatever you decide is fine."

A tiny frown had appeared between her

brows. His heart nearly stopped when she shook her head.

"I'm sorry."

He figured the pain in his chest must be from his heart ripping in two. "Is there anything I can do?"

"I want to marry for love," she replied, "not for the fantasy wedding with the designer dress and the row of bridesmaids. That's not important."

Could a man die from despair? Mitch wondered.

"I'd marry you at city hall, or in Las Vegas, or on a mountaintop if that's what you want, because I do love you," she said.

Had he heard right? Had she just accepted his proposal? Her face blurred before his eyes and he had to blink several times, holding tight to her hand as though it were an anchor as he got to his feet.

"All I want," he told her as he wrapped his arms around her, "is to make you as happy as you've just made me." He gazed into her upturned face. "Beautiful," he murmured, "inside and out."

And then he kissed her. When he finally came up for air, she was smiling.

"Tell me one thing," she said. "Why are you wearing a football uniform?"

"Halloween," he replied with a grin. "And because I just threw the winning pass."

Liz touched his cheek. "Translation, please."

"I love you, too," he replied. "Always and forever."

* * * * *

YES! Please send me **The Montana Mavericks Collection** in Larger Print. This collection begins with 3 FREE books and 2 FREE gifts (gifts valued at approx. $20.00 retail) in the first shipment, along with the other first 4 books from the collection! If I do not cancel, I will receive 8 monthly shipments until I have the entire 51-book Montana Mavericks collection. I will receive 2 or 3 FREE books in each shipment and I will pay just $4.99 US/ $5.89 CDN for each of the other four books in each shipment, plus $2.99 for shipping and handling per shipment.*If I decide to keep the entire collection, I'll have paid for only 32 books, because 19 books are FREE! I understand that accepting the 3 free books and gifts places me under no obligation to buy anything. I can always return a shipment and cancel at any time. My free books and gifts are mine to keep no matter what I decide.

263 HCN 2404   463 HCN 2404

Name	(PLEASE PRINT)	
Address		Apt. #
City	State/Prov.	Zip/Postal Code

Signature (if under 18, a parent or guardian must sign)

Mail to the **Reader Service:**

IN U.S.A.: P.O. Box 1867, Buffalo, NY 14240-1867
IN CANADA: P.O. Box 609, Fort Erie, Ontario L2A 5X3

* Terms and prices subject to change without notice. Prices do not include applicable taxes. Sales tax applicable in N.Y. Canadian residents will be charged applicable taxes. This offer is limited to one order per household. All orders subject to approval. Credit or debit balances in a customer's account(s) may be offset by any other outstanding balance owed by or to the customer. Please allow 4 to 6 weeks for delivery. Offer available while quantities last. Offer not available to Quebec residents.

Your Privacy—The Reader Service is committed to protecting your privacy. Our Privacy Policy is available online at www.ReaderService.com or upon request from the Reader Service.

We make a portion of our mailing list available to reputable third parties that offer products we believe may interest you. If you prefer that we not exchange your name with third parties, or if you wish to clarify or modify your communication preferences, please visit us at www.ReaderService.com/consumerschoice or write to us at Reader Service Preference Service, P.O. Box 9062, Buffalo, NY 14269. Include your complete name and address.

REQUEST YOUR FREE BOOKS!

2 FREE NOVELS PLUS 2 FREE GIFTS!

⟨H⟩ HARLEQUIN®

SPECIAL EDITION

Life, Love & Family

YES! Please send me 2 FREE Harlequin® Special Edition novels and my 2 FREE gifts (gifts are worth about $10). After receiving them, if I don't wish to receive any more books, I can return the shipping statement marked "cancel." If I don't cancel, I will receive 6 brand-new novels every month and be billed just $4.74 per book in the U.S. or $5.24 per book in Canada. That's a savings of at least 14% off the cover price! It's quite a bargain! Shipping and handling is just 50¢ per book in the U.S. and 75¢ per book in Canada.* I understand that accepting the 2 free books and gifts places me under no obligation to buy anything. I can always return a shipment and cancel at any time. Even if I never buy another book, the two free books and gifts are mine to keep forever.

235/335 HDN F46C

Name _____ (PLEASE PRINT) _____

Address _____ Apt. # _____

City _____ State/Prov. _____ Zip/Postal Code _____

Signature (if under 18, a parent or guardian must sign) _____

Mail to the **Harlequin® Reader Service:**
IN U.S.A.: P.O. Box 1867, Buffalo, NY 14240-1867
IN CANADA: P.O. Box 609, Fort Erie, Ontario L2A 5X3

Want to try two free books from another line?
Call 1-800-873-8635 or visit www.ReaderService.com.

* Terms and prices subject to change without notice. Prices do not include applicable taxes. Sales tax applicable in N.Y. Canadian residents will be charged applicable taxes. Offer not valid in Quebec. This offer is limited to one order per household. Not valid for current subscribers to Harlequin Special Edition books. All orders subject to credit approval. Credit or debit balances in a customer's account(s) may be offset by any other outstanding balance owed by or to the customer. Please allow 4 to 6 weeks for delivery. Offer available while quantities last.

Your Privacy—The Harlequin® Reader Service is committed to protecting your privacy. Our Privacy Policy is available online at www.ReaderService.com or upon request from the Harlequin Reader Service.

We make a portion of our mailing list available to reputable third parties that offer products we believe may interest you. If you prefer that we not exchange your name with third parties, or if you wish to clarify or modify your communication preferences, please visit us at www.ReaderService.com/consumerchoice or write to us at Harlequin Reader Service Preference Service, P.O. Box 9062, Buffalo, NY 14269. Include your complete name and address.

HSEDIR13R

REQUEST YOUR FREE BOOKS!
2 FREE NOVELS PLUS 2 FREE GIFTS!

LOVE, HOME & HAPPINESS

YES! Please send me 2 FREE Harlequin® American Romance® novels and my 2 FREE gifts (gifts are worth about $10). After receiving them, if I don't wish to receive any more books, I can return the shipping statement marked "cancel." If I don't cancel, I will receive 4 brand-new novels every month and be billed just $4.74 per book in the U.S. or $5.24 per book in Canada. That's a savings of at least 14% off the cover price! It's quite a bargain! Shipping and handling is just 50¢ per book in the U.S. and 75¢ per book in Canada.* I understand that accepting the 2 free books and gifts places me under no obligation to buy anything. I can always return a shipment and cancel at any time. Even if I never buy another book, the two free books and gifts are mine to keep forever.

154/354 HDN F4YY

Name _____ (PLEASE PRINT)

Address _____ Apt. # _____

City _____ State/Prov. _____ Zip/Postal Code _____

Signature (if under 18, a parent or guardian must sign)

Mail to the **Harlequin® Reader Service:**
IN U.S.A.: P.O. Box 1867, Buffalo, NY 14240-1867
IN CANADA: P.O. Box 609, Fort Erie, Ontario L2A 5X3

Want to try two free books from another line?
Call 1-800-873-8635 or visit www.ReaderService.com.

* Terms and prices subject to change without notice. Prices do not include applicable taxes. Sales tax applicable in N.Y. Canadian residents will be charged applicable taxes. Offer not valid in Quebec. This offer is limited to one order per household. Not valid for current subscribers to Harlequin American Romance books. All orders subject to credit approval. Credit or debit balances in a customer's account(s) may be offset by any other outstanding balance owed by or to the customer. Please allow 4 to 6 weeks for delivery. Offer available while quantities last.

Your Privacy—The Harlequin® Reader Service is committed to protecting your privacy. Our Privacy Policy is available online at www.ReaderService.com or upon request from the Harlequin Reader Service.

We make a portion of our mailing list available to reputable third parties that offer products we believe may interest you. If you prefer that we not exchange your name with third parties, or if you wish to clarify or modify your communication preferences, please visit us at www.ReaderService.com/consumerchoice or write to us at Harlequin Reader Service Preference Service, P.O. Box 9062, Buffalo, NY 14269. Include your complete name and address.

HARDIR13R